S0-BYJ-483

WRAPPED IN INK

A MONTGOMERY INK: BOULDER NOVEL

CARRIE ANN RYAN

Wrapped in Ink
A Montgomery Ink: Boulder Novel
By: Carrie Ann Ryan
© 2019 Carrie Ann Ryan
ISBN: 978-1-947007-47-5

Cover Art by Charity Hendry
Photograph by Wander Photography

This book is licensed for your personal enjoyment only. This book may not be re-sold or given away to other people. If you would like to share this book with another person, please purchase an additional copy for each person or use proper retail channels to lend a copy. If you're reading this book and did not purchase it, or it was not purchased for your use only, then please return it and purchase your own copy. Thank you for respecting the hard work of this author.
All characters in this book are fiction and figments of the author's imagination.

PRAISE FOR CARRIE ANN RYAN

"Carrie Ann Ryan knows how to pull your heartstrings and make your pulse pound! Her wonderful Redwood Pack series will draw you in and keep you reading long into the night. I can't wait to see what comes next with the new generation, the Talons. Keep them coming, Carrie Ann!" –Lara Adrian, New York Times bestselling author of CRAVE THE NIGHT

"Carrie Ann Ryan never fails to draw readers in with passion, raw sensuality, and characters that pop off the page. Any book by Carrie Ann is an absolute treat." – New York Times Bestselling Author J. Kenner

"With snarky humor, sizzling love scenes, and brilliant, imaginative worldbuilding, The Dante's Circle series reads as if Carrie Ann Ryan peeked at my personal wish list!" – NYT Bestselling Author, Larissa Ione

"Carrie Ann Ryan writes sexy shifters in a world full of passionate happily-ever-afters." – New York Times Bestselling Author Vivian Arend

"Carrie Ann's books are sexy with characters you can't help but love from page one. They are heat and heart blended to perfection." New York Times Bestselling Author Jayne Rylon

Carrie Ann Ryan's books are wickedly funny and deliciously hot, with plenty of twists to keep you guessing. They'll keep you up all night!" USA Today Bestselling Author Cari Quinn

"Once again, Carrie Ann Ryan knocks the Dante's Circle series out of the park. The queen of hot, sexy, enthralling paranormal romance, Carrie Ann is an author not to miss!" *New York Times* bestselling Author Marie Harte

DEDICATION

To Mom, Dad, and K.
Thank you for taking this journey with me.
For being my home.
For showing me what it means to find peace.

WRAPPED IN INK

The Montgomery Ink saga continues with a new series set in Boulder, where a family secret might just change everything.

One mistake at a friend's wedding rocks Liam Montgomery's entire world, and everything he thought was true turns out to be a lie. But when an accident lands him in the ER, Liam meets someone that might just be the distraction he needs.

Arden Brady has spent her life in and out of hospitals. But according to the world, she doesn't look sick. She's lost jobs and friends because they don't see beneath the surface, but she's learned to rely on her family and herself to keep going. And then she meets Liam.

With two sets of overprotective siblings and a puppy

that can't help but get into everything, Liam and Arden might just fall harder than either one ever expected.

CHAPTER 1

*L*iam Montgomery leaned against the wall and did his best to stay out of the way. It wasn't easy since, like the rest of his family, he was broad and tall and tended to stand out amongst the crowd—that is, unless the crowd was full of Montgomerys. Then, he blended in.

Today, however, only a fraction of the Montgomerys were here—his immediate family—and not what felt like tens of thousands of cousins, uncles, and aunts that lived in the state.

Liam looked over the crush of wedding goers as they milled around with their pre-ceremony drinks and tried to spot his family. The Boulder Montgomerys had been invited to his friends' wedding and had all shown up, which was nice, considering that though they all lived in the same city, they were rarely in the same place unless there was a family dinner.

Those didn't come often these days since they were all busier than usual, but Liam had a feeling that once his mom saw all her ducklings in one place, there would be an edict for a dinner sometime soon.

Liam sipped the last of his beer and then looked around for a tray to set it down on since he was finished. He nodded at an attendant as they took his bottle and then leaned back against the wall. He never really understood why someone needed a drink before a wedding unless you were the one getting married, but he didn't really mind that he could have a beer while waiting for everything to start.

"Why are you over here sulking?" Bristol asked as she came to his side and leaned into him. Liam wrapped his arms around his little sister's shoulders and kissed the top of her head. She let out a strangled noise, and he knew that she was rolling her eyes at him even though he couldn't see her face just then.

"Really? Really?" She sounded so annoyed that Liam couldn't help but grin.

He turned to face her. "What? You're my baby sister. I'm allowed to do things like that." He reached out to mess with her hair again, and she pulled away, huffing.

"I'm in my thirties. You don't have to coddle me and

kiss me on the top of the head like I'm still wearing braids."

Liam narrowed his eyes and then traced his finger along one of the tiny braids in her updo. "Um, I beg to differ with the whole braids thing."

She glared at him and then flipped him off. "It's two tiny little braids in my updo that the hairstylist had fun with. I'm not actually in pigtails. Stop treating me like a baby."

"I'm always going to treat you like a baby. Because you're my baby sister."

"You don't treat Aaron like you do me, and he's younger than I am."

"He might be, and I do treat him like a baby brother. But you're still the wee little girl."

She flipped him off and then winced as their parents' voices hit them. "Did I just see you flipping off your brother at a very fancy event?" Francine Montgomery asked as she came up to stand by them, tapping her daughter on the nose.

"Surely, we did not," Timothy Montgomery asserted, holding back a grin.

Considering that both of Liam's parents flipped each other off constantly, as did the rest of the Montgomery family, Liam knew that it was all bluster. But mothering Bristol or any of them was sort of what their mom did. And he knew she loved it.

"Liam started it," Bristol said, and Liam burst out laughing.

"Oh, yes, that's the mature sister I know and love," he added as Bristol punched him in the gut.

He let out an *oof* and rubbed his stomach.

"You're packing a punch there, baby sister," he muttered.

Bristol coughed and used her hands to cover up the middle finger she used to flip him off with again.

"I still saw that, young lady. And you shouldn't hit your brother like that," their mother added. Liam just shook his head.

He loved his family, he really did. But, sometimes, it felt like they were in their own little comedy show outside of the world, a place where nothing mattered but them. And he was fine with that. They had always been there for him. They were the true friends and close relatives he'd had all his life.

Liam was a Montgomery, just like the rest of them. They had connections and ties that never died, no matter how much they made fun of each other or flipped each other off. Because they were family, and that's what mattered most.

As his brothers came walking in, grinning at him and Bristol, Liam leaned back against the wall and looked at them all.

Ethan was only a couple of years younger than Liam and brilliant. He didn't understand half the things that Ethan talked about when he spoke about his job, but that didn't matter. His brother was just that damn good at everything. And Aaron? Aaron was brilliant in his own way. He might not be science and math smart like Ethan, but the art that he created was breathtaking, and Liam knew it would last into the ages.

Just like Bristol's music would.

They were all so damn talented and amazing. And while he sometimes felt a little left behind, he knew he shouldn't. Because he liked his job, and he was damn good at it. He'd even liked it when he was a model back in the day, even though everyone had made fun of him for it.

But it had made him enough money to get him through college. With some left over to help the rest of his family so nobody ended up in debt.

If he had to deal with being called "pretty boy" and made fun of for his looks? He'd take it.

And he'd flip off his family as he did.

"What are we doing over here?" Aaron asked, frowning. "Is there some kind of Montgomery reunion I wasn't aware of?"

"I'm just so happy that all of our family is together in one place," Francine said, sliding in between Liam's two brothers and wrapping her arms around their waists. "Y'all are getting so big."

Liam snorted. "Um, Mom? I think we've all gone way past the whole growing up stage. We're pretty much as big as we're gonna get."

"I don't know, Liam, I think Bristol might one day actually grow up and reach normal height at some point." Ethan winked and patted Bristol on the head.

Their baby sister narrowed her eyes and used both fingers this time, raising them high into the air. She quickly lowered them as Francine and Timothy glared at her.

"At least *try* to act like we're not all heathens," Timothy said, although he laughed as he did. "We're supposed to be the nice family at a beautiful wedding, not people flipping each other off just because we can. It gets kind of old after a while."

"That is true," Liam added. He was surprised that Bristol didn't flip him off again.

"If everyone would stop touching my hair, though, that would be amazing," Bristol added.

"Your hair does look lovely, dear," Francine said, studying her daughter. "Did Zia do it?"

Liam met his brothers' gazes and held back a grin.

It didn't matter how long Zia and Bristol had been broken up, their mother wanted marriages for her children. And babies. And so, the fact that Bristol and her ex-girlfriend were still friends always gave Francine hope.

Besides, it took the attention off the rest of them so they weren't constantly being asked when they were going to settle down and find a nice boy or girl to marry. Liam wasn't ready for that, and after he had witnessed all the trouble and heartache that his cousins had gone through in their marriages, he was okay waiting that out for a little while. He had time. Lots of time.

The fact that he was thinking all of this at his friends' wedding wasn't lost on him. Craig and Cain had been through their own hells, but were now going to say their vows to each other and then head off into the sunset, happily married. Maybe they'd eventually adopt a baby because they were on the right path for that.

Liam was fine on his own road, thank you very much.

"Zia didn't do my hair, Mom," Bristol said, and Liam knew she was holding back a sigh. "She's not even in town."

"But did she help you with the style or something? She's just so amazing with all her techniques and things. I follow her on Instagram, you know? She's getting her own makeup line and everything. Did you know that, Bristol?"

Zia was an Instagram beauty blogger who was getting her own product line or something like that. Liam was the one who had introduced her to Bristol since he used to model with her back in the day. It was still a little weird to think that his baby sister had exes in her life. He tried not to think of Bristol as someone who could actually have a relationship. But Zia had been good. Not right for Bristol, but good.

"I know, Mom. Zia and her boyfriend are out of town on vacation, though." Bristol emphasized the word *boyfriend*, and their mother's face fell.

"Oh, I didn't know she was seeing someone."

"Has been for a few months now. I think I hear wedding bells."

"Speaking of wedding bells," Ethan put in. "We should probably find our seats, or Craig and Cain will beat the crap out of us for ruining their wedding."

"Yeah, we can't ruin another one," Aaron put in and then laughed.

"What wedding have we ruined?"

"I'm sure we ruined a few," Aaron put in, waving his hand.

Liam laughed and put his arms around Bristol's shoulders as they all walked into the seating area. "I'm sure our mere presence does that. They can't help but be intimidated by us. We are the Montgomerys, after all."

"They're probably just intimidated by you, pretty boy," Ethan said, ducking out of the way as Liam tried to punch him.

"Boys," their mom said in that voice that had been the

same since they were little. One word and they all stopped.

Even Bristol froze.

"Sorry," they all mumbled under their breaths and then looked at each other, grinning.

No, they weren't kids anymore, nowhere close, actually, but sometimes, it was good to be near family. Liam took a seat at the end of the bench with Bristol sitting next to him, and then Ethan, Aaron, and their parents. Liam had met Cain back in his modeling days, and the two of them had struck up a friendship that had lasted through the years.

Yeah, Liam had been a teenage model, and it continued into his twenties. He'd made a shit ton of money but then left that life as quickly as he could. Somehow, he hadn't found his way into drugs or too much drinking or getting a disease from all the women he could have slept with over that time. A few of his friends back in the day had succumbed to exactly that. It didn't matter what decade you were in, it felt like the craze of wanting to do something bad and be in that circle just kept coming at you.

Liam had then met Craig in his *new* job. Liam had been at his agency in New York, meeting his representative for a new book deal when Craig had come out, muttering about authors and lattes and something else. Craig had been an intern at the time and was now a full-time editor at Liam's publishing house—not *his* editor since Maisie would never let him go. Liam had struck up a conversation with Craig when they were both waiting for a meeting.

Then he'd introduced Craig to Cain, and the two of them had hit it off.

They'd also come to visit Liam enough times in Colorado that they had finally bought another home in the Rockies.

And so, they'd decided to get married and have their ceremony in the mountains of Boulder, rather than in the city on the east coast.

Liam figured that the couple would probably have another party out in New York, but that was fine with him. He might just hop on a plane and fly out there for that, too. He liked the two grooms, and they deserved this and much more.

However, the way his mother kept looking around at all the wedding decorations and everything else, he had a feeling that this was simply one more nail in the coffin of his bachelorhood.

Not that he was actively against getting married, he just hadn't found the right person yet. None of the Montgomerys in this city had.

But his mother was determined to have her way and make sure that the wedding bells never ceased.

A Montgomery wedding was what she wanted. And,

apparently, it was what she was going to get, no matter the cost.

At least that's what she had said at their last family dinner, causing his siblings and him to burst out laughing.

It was like she was waging war, and weddings and babies were the only way to end it.

Well, she'd have to wait a bit longer. Because today was about Craig and Cain, not the Montgomerys. Even if it felt like they were the center of their own world sometimes.

The music started, and Liam just leaned back onto the bench and looked around. They were outdoors, the sun shining, and the mountains gleaming against the blue sky. Didn't matter what season it was, even if it was freezing outside, the sky could still be blue. And then he figured that a snowstorm or a thunderstorm would likely come out of nowhere and drench everyone, but they had these few precious moments. And they were going to take them.

Craig and Cain looked hot as hell in their matching tuxes and grins. Liam shook his head when Cain dipped Craig into a very intense, very not-wedding-like kiss.

There were hoots and hollers, mostly by him and his brothers, and Bristol wiped her tears, laughed, and looked on with the rest of the crowd as the two men began the next phase of their lives together.

"That was so beautiful," Francine said, wiping her face. "I just can't wait to see what happens at your weddings."

"Mom," Liam sighed.

"What? I have four beautiful children, and none of them want to be married. None of you are actually in relationships. What have I done wrong?"

"Do you ever feel like she was born in the wrong century?" Bristol asked, tapping her chin.

"You mean that she's like a Regency momma, watching her little ducklings not able to find their duke or their lord at a ballroom?" Ethan asked.

"Yes, I think we're all wallflowers here," Bristol said, sounding so serious that he almost thought she meant it. Then he looked in her eyes and saw the laughter.

"There's nothing wallflower about you, Bristol."

"Oh, that's so sweet. Seriously. But again, I don't really want to get married right now. You know, I would kind of need a boyfriend or a girlfriend to make that happen."

"Well, don't say that too loudly, or you know Mom will just fly someone out to find you." Ethan shook his head and grinned. "I swear she's going to start setting us up on blind dates or bringing people to family dinners if we don't start pairing off soon."

"That may be true, but Bristol would be first, right?" Liam asked quickly.

"Oh, no. I'm not going first. You're the eldest. You're the one who gets to get married."

"No, don't the dukes and the sons of dukes get to wait until their little baby sister is presented for her opening and pushed out into the real world without a net?" Liam asked and then paused. "Is the word opening? What is the word?"

"Debut," Aaron said, and everybody looked at him. "What? I happen to know a few women who read historical romance."

They all *kept* looking.

"Okay, just because Lisa Kleypas is one of my favorite authors does not mean I lose my man card."

They all started laughing, and Bristol hugged Aaron hard.

"I think that makes you the best. Because her Wallflower series is seriously one of my favorites ever."

"I know, right?" Aaron asked. Liam just looked at Ethan before they both cracked up laughing.

It was good to be with the family. Good to be smiling and acting as if they all weren't sometimes stressed with their jobs or the fact that their mom really wanted them to settle down. It was good not to think about anything but being with the people that mattered the most. His family.

The four of them stood off to the side near the outside of the building where there was some restoration work being done, trying to stay out of the way. They tended to be loud, and this was about Craig and Cain and their day, so none of them really wanted to be the center of attention.

Nor did they want to be near the group when ties and garters were being thrown in place of bouquets.

Liam knew that his mother was probably hunting for them since the time for the toss was almost upon them, so they were hiding.

A little.

Liam looked up when he heard a scratching sound and frowned. "What was that?" he said, his voice soft.

"What was what?" Bristol asked, and then her eyes widened. "Liam!"

Liam looked to the right and then threw himself over his little sister as the scaffolding that had been right beside them fell. There was a sharp pain, and a deafening crunch as he heard his little sister scream, his brothers shout to him, and then he heard no more.

There was only darkness.

Nothing.

CHAPTER 2

*A*rden Brady leaned back on the bed and did her best not to glare at her oppressive brothers. It wasn't their fault that they were overbearing, overprotective, and over…everything. They were only trying to be helpful. At least, that's what she told herself for the umpteenth time.

They were *always* just trying to be helpful.

She was twenty-eight years old and the youngest of five. Her four older brothers still thought of her as the baby and made sure that whenever they interacted with her, she knew that.

And considering that the bed she was currently in was a *hospital* bed, maybe they had a reason. A reason they had to deal with much too often.

Too bad strangling all four of them would take skills Arden didn't have—and was illegal. Far too public while she was in the emergency room getting treatment. Best to murder them all when they came to her house after she got out of the hospital. She knew they'd all come with her to tuck her in and wait on her like she was a child instead of a grown woman who had a tiny little disease with symptoms that sometimes came out of the woodwork to ruin her plans.

"Are you sure we can't get you anything?" Cross asked, staring at her.

"I'm fine. Stop glaring." She paused, hating how tired she sounded. She was always tired these days. "Please." She closed her eyes, ignoring the pain in her arm where the IV worked its magic.

"I'm not glaring," Cross said, indeed glaring.

"You kind of are," Prior added, peering at Cross.

"I don't know, I think that's his normal face," Macon put in.

"Well, then his normal is pretty much a glare," Nate said, grinning.

Arden closed her eyes and prayed for peace. Peace from pain, peace from the annoyance of having to be in the hospital after an almost perfect day, and peace from her brothers. Because while they were all grown men and very overprotective and annoying at times, they also tended to bicker with each other like they were ten years old rather than in their thirties.

"Really, you're glaring. All of you are. I'm fine. You can go and finish your days. I'll just be here getting an infusion. We've been here before, right?"

"Yeah, we have. So, we're not going to leave." Cross finally took a seat in the chair next to her bed. Her other brothers were already sitting, each trying to look calm and casual even though she knew none of them were.

"It should only take another couple of hours. Seriously, enjoy the day. It's sunny and beautiful out."

"We know it's sunny, hence why you're in the damn bed," Prior snapped. And then he closed his eyes and shook his head. "Sorry, Arden."

"Don't be sorry. I'm as pissed off as you are. This sucks. I can't go and have a nice day out in the sun, even with all the sunscreen in the world and a hat. Instead, I get a stupid rash from the heat and the freaking sun itself."

"You're sick, it's not only a rash," Macon whispered.

Arden lifted up her good arm and pointed at the IV in her other elbow. "Oh, I know. The fact that I'm getting an IV and not just putting on aloe tells me so. But it's lupus, you guys. It's never going away. We're just going to have to deal. I am."

"No, it's never going away. And neither are we. So, you're going to have to deal with us watching over you."

"Please, don't. Please just go and let me be." She lay her head on the pillow and really wished they would leave her alone. She loved them. Adored them more than anything in the world except for maybe her dog, yet she was done with it all.

It had been a nice, unusually warm day for the season, so all of them had decided to go to an outdoor concert. She'd slathered herself up with sunscreen, put on a hat, and done her best to enjoy the day. Because doing that sometimes wasn't easy when you had a disease that no one could actually see you had.

"So, do you think that nurse is here?" Prior said, grinning even though it didn't completely reach his eyes.

Arden snorted and looked over at her brother. "I think she's married, Prior."

"Nope, divorced," Macon put in. They all looked at him, and he just shrugged. "What? I know things."

"I swear you can figure out and find single women within a five-mile radius no matter where you are. We could be in a completely isolated forest with no humans around, and you'd still find a direct path to the single women."

Macon grinned. "It's a skill I have."

"Pretty much your only skill," Nate muttered, and the two of them playfully punched at each other. A single hit each. Arden just rolled her eyes. They were trying to make her laugh and smile. They didn't always act this immature, but if they needed to make her smile, this is what they did. But she hated that they were all so good at this. Loathed the fact that she knew that Cross had already called their parents to let them know that their baby girl was once again in the hospital.

It didn't matter that Arden's parents had moved out to Virginia and were thousands of miles away. They worried just as much as the rest of them. Arden would always be weak, need to be cared for. And she resented it. She knew that everyone loved her, understood that they only wanted her to be healthy and okay. But that wasn't going to happen. It was never going to happen.

And with everything else going on in her life, even with how small and frail those things seemed in comparison to her disease, she knew she should hold onto the fact that her family still loved her and cared for her and wanted to make sure she was okay.

Because she knew what would happen as time moved on, as her disease grew. People would walk away, get tired of her being the sick girl because that's all they saw. It'd happened before. Even if they couldn't see the actual disease, didn't see a cane or a wheelchair to let them know that she was virtually disabled, they *could* see the results of what happened when her body attacked itself.

They could see it by her not being there. By her canceling on parties or just walking away when she got too tired.

Most saw her as lazy or boring.

Her brothers never had. They'd always been there for her. And now she was grumbling over the fact that they were here for her when no one else was?

Cross was in front of her, wiping tears from her face before she even realized that she had started crying.

"Should we call the nurse? Get you some pain meds?"

She shook her head and then curled into a fetal position on the bed.

"I'm not in pain."

All four brothers glared at her.

"Not more pain than usual. Just thinking and feeling sad. Maybe I need a book or something." But she knew she wasn't going to be able to read. Even her eyes hurt today.

She had gone out with her brothers and ended up getting sick from the sun. So, they had given her fluids and meds to treat the symptoms. Because the sun had given her a rash and made her feel terrible. And she wasn't even allergic to the damn thing.

It caused cramps all over her body, spasms that were attacking her joints, her skin, and even her hair at the moment.

It'd also done some uncomfortable things to her digestive system, stuff she was not going to talk about with her brothers. They had seen enough evidence of it in her life as it was. She was completely done talking to them about it.

Her siblings had seen her at her weakest, and she was afraid that they were never going to see her strong again.

"I'm going to get the nurse," Prior put in, standing up. Arden looked up at him and grinned, even though it hurt her face to do so.

"You just want to get her number," she said, smiling a little easier. "But do it for me."

"I'm not sharing a woman with you, Arden."

"I'm not saying you should, dork," she said with a laugh.

"She's all yours, Prior," Cross said, his eyes dancing with laughter. They all knew that Prior was doing this to make them smile and laugh after a hard day, and Arden was happy about it. Because spending one's day in the ER because there were no beds upstairs in the ward where she normally got her treatment wasn't really what any of them had planned.

But she knew they all loved her, even if they were going to annoy the hell out of her for the rest of the day —and probably the week. And she loved them, too.

"You know what? I'm going to see if there's a way we can get you into a private room," Nate said, standing up, as well.

Arden shook her head. "I'm fine. You're the ones taking up all the space."

"We're big, we tend to do that," Macon said, leaning back in his chair and stretching his legs out into the hallway. One of the nurses glared at him, and he quickly pulled his feet in. The woman had to be all of five feet, and she had scared Arden's big brother. Good. He needed that.

"I don't need a private room." Plus, because they would have to admit her if they moved her upstairs, insurance wouldn't cover something like that. She did not even want to think about her bill as it was. She was self-employed, and that meant medical insurance was a bitch. The copay for this was going to be insane even though she'd already met her deductible for the year.

"That hospital bed right next to you near the door isn't going to stay empty for long," Cross muttered. "But you're right, I guess you'll be fine here." He met her gaze, and she knew he was thinking exactly what she was. Money sucked when it came to medical issues. Didn't matter how much she saved, or how much she made. Didn't matter how much her family helped her—because they helped her a lot even though it grated on her pride. Medical bills just kept coming.

But she didn't want to think about that right then. Instead, she stretched her legs as much as she could, ignoring the pain since she knew that she needed to move around as much as she was able, and just closed her eyes for a bit.

She didn't know how long she napped, but eventually, she opened her eyes and saw that she was not alone in this part of the ER anymore. Instead, there was a man there with his arm bandaged, and an IV in his other arm, connected to a blood bag. He looked as if he had already gotten his stitches and everything, but he was still stuck in a bed like she was. It'd never made much sense to her that people were required to stay in the ER for longer than necessary, meaning others were forced to sit in the waiting room until there were available beds. But this was the busiest hospital in the area—and the smallest. And that meant that sometimes things just didn't make sense.

But the nurses and the doctors and the rest of the staff worked their butts off. Arden had been here more times than she could count, and she could always rely on anyone that worked here. The nurses knew her by name, even if they sometimes had to blink a few times to remember exactly who she was. But everyone on staff was always caring, hardworking, and never, like that one sentator had thought, played a game of cards.

Arden smiled then, and the man in the other bed looked at her and grinned back.

She held back a wince since she hadn't really meant to smile at him, but she couldn't help it. Because, that man? Handsome as fuck.

He looked vaguely familiar, but only in that really-hot-guy sort of way.

He had a strong jaw, bright hazel eyes, and chiseled cheekbones that looked as if they could cut granite.

His hair flopped over his forehead just a little—long on the top, short on the sides.

And even in a hospital gown, he looked damn sexy.

He had a blanket over his legs so she couldn't see exactly how muscular he was, and she was glad for it. Perving on a fellow patient really wasn't the best thing.

She turned away and looked around for her brothers, embarrassed that she had been caught looking at him.

She frowned, realizing her siblings had left her alone. Had that ever happened before?

"The guys you were with just walked out," the man to her left said, and she startled before turning to him. "Excuse me?" She did her best to sound normal—not that she wasn't normal, but she really wasn't very good at social situations. It didn't help that she worked from home and didn't have a lot of friends. Or *any* friends besides her dog. But, anyway, that wasn't important right then.

"You were sleeping when they rolled me back here, but there were four guys in here earlier. Three of them said they were heading out to do something, and the biggest one got a phone call and had to leave the room since we're not allowed to be on our phones in here." The man shrugged. "He sort of glared at me before he walked out, so I don't know if he wanted me to not talk to you, or let you know where they went. Didn't leave a note or anything I don't think."

Arden blinked at him, wondering why he was talking so much. Nobody spoke to her. She was really good in her little bubble of social awkwardness, not dealing with people.

But he was just so...pretty. She was very, very bad at this whole thing.

"I'm Liam, by the way. Liam Montgomery."

"Oh." She cleared her throat. "Arden. I'm Arden Brady. And those four big guys are my brothers."

"So, not your boyfriend? Or boyfriends? Of course, that's not as weird as it sounds."

Her eyebrows shot up. "No, definitely not my boyfriends. Not even a little. Plus, four?"

"Yeah, four might be a lot. But I have a cousin who has two husbands, so it's not that uncommon."

Arden swallowed hard, trying not to think about exactly what she would do with two Liams. Because, dear God. Two Liams? She didn't even know the man. But he was just so pretty. And, apparently, she had gotten some pain meds with the rest of her IV. She wasn't normally this loopy. Dear God, she couldn't focus.

"Oh, well, that's good." She sighed. "Sorry, I'm still a little groggy from my nap. No, those were my brothers.

And good for your cousin. Two husbands? I don't even have one."

Liam smiled. "Good to know."

Was he flirting? He was actually flirting with her. What did she look like? Oh, yeah, now she remembered. She had a butterfly rash on her cheeks, more on her neck, and all down the left side of her body. Plus, her stomach hurt, and she knew she was probably going to make a mess of herself soon if she didn't find a restroom. Thank you, cramping and lupus. Dear God, she hated her life.

But she was going to ignore all of that and pretend that she wasn't in pain. Disregard the needle shoved into her arm right then, giving her fluids. She was going to flirt right back and pretend that she wasn't a mess.

Because, dear God, Arden was a mess.

"So, what are you in for?" Liam asked, leaning back into the bed.

"Oh, just meds and fluids. Got a little too much sun today."

It wasn't that she was really hiding the fact that she had lupus, but it wasn't the easiest thing to tell people. Most didn't know anything about it, and it wasn't easy to explain since the symptoms were the same as about a dozen other things.

But considering that she'd had it since she was eighteen, she knew damn well that she had it. She had a whole host of other symptoms too, though, and was constantly being diagnosed with other things on top of the lupus.

And explaining that to a cute guy she was probably never going to see again? Not really on her list of priorities.

"Well, I hope you get better soon." He said the words, and from his expression, it looked like he meant them. Weird. She wasn't used to people actually talking to her.

"So, what are *you* in for?"

"A piece of scaffolding fell on me and my sister while we were at a wedding." He lifted up his arm and winced. "Got a few stitches, and because of what it nicked, I get to get a nice bag of blood." He pointed up to the bag and paled ever so slightly.

"Not a fan of blood?"

"Not really. Didn't really realize it until just now. They were going to admit me, but things got backed up, so they're doing things in the ER."

"Same," Arden said. "How's your sister?" she asked quickly, hating that she hadn't asked right away.

"Bristol is fine. Not even a bruise. Even though I threw her to the ground kind of hard when I jumped on top of her."

He had thrown himself over his little sister's body to protect her from scaffolding? Dear God, this man was just...everything. Maybe she was dreaming. A lupus-treatment-induced fantasy. If so, she didn't want to wake up. She was fine with Liam Montgomery.

"You'll be okay, though?" he asked, looking concerned.

"I'll be fine." At least as fine as she ever was. But she didn't qualify that.

"Good."

"And you?"

"I got knocked out for like ten seconds, but they said I didn't get a concussion. I think I scared my brain more than anything else," he said with a laugh. "So, they might keep me overnight if they can get me a room. Or I'll stay here for a bit. Or maybe go home. It's pretty much up to the doctors at this point."

"Isn't it always?" she asked, laughing sadly.

"Very true. But I guess the scenery isn't too bad."

She just raised a brow at that before he continued. "Sorry. I'm not usually this bad at the whole flirting thing."

"You must be pretty hard up if you're flirting with me in an ER." She hadn't meant to say that, but now that it was out there, she pointed at the rash on her face. "I mean, really?"

"I think you're pretty cute," he said, shrugging and then wincing since she knew he had probably moved the IV a bit.

Cute. That was everything she'd ever dreamed of. Arden Brady, the cute one. The only sister. The sick one.

Well, at least cute was better than sick. She'd take it.

"I'd say thank you. But…cute?"

"Give me a break, I'm in a hospital gown here. I'm not really at my best."

"Same. But thanks for making me smile," she said, genuinely meaning it.

"Thanks for making me do the same. And considering I can hear a group of people, either your family or mine is on their way."

Arden strained to listen and then heard what sounded like a stampede of feet. "How many family members do you have?" she asked, a little weary.

"Two brothers, a sister, and two parents. Plus, for all I know, some of the wedding party is here, too. And, let's not talk about the cousins. Dear Lord, the cousins."

She snorted then and shook her head. "Well, it seems we both come from big families."

"See? Another thing in common."

"And what was the first?"

"I would say both of us sitting here in a hospital bed like we are could count as the first one."

"Maybe."

She grinned, listening to him speak, and felt lighter than she had in a long time. Yeah, her body hurt, her joints ached, and her hair felt like it was on fire, but feeling like she was normal for just a moment? That was priceless.

So, whoever this Liam Montgomery was, she was going to thank him. Even if she never saw him again after today. Because she probably wouldn't. That wasn't her luck.

It never was.

CHAPTER 3

*L*iam winced as he tried to get comfortable in his bed. Arden reached out as if to help him, but most likely realized that she too was confined by the tubes and machines.

"Are you okay?" Arden asked and shook her head. "Sorry. I know you aren't, but, yeah..." Then she smiled. The expression went right to her eyes, and Liam couldn't help but notice that even with the rash, the evident exhaustion, and whatever else was going on with her, she was beautiful.

Who knew that he'd find someone like her in a place like this? Wasn't the best place to pick up a woman, but he'd had a hell of a day, and he might as well enjoy himself. And if he could make her smile like that again, he'd keep doing it.

Her honey-blond hair, while pulled back at the nape of her neck, still tumbled over her shoulder, and he wanted to reach out and see if it was as soft as it looked. Not that he would since he just met her. But, still.

Her face, still covered by a rash on one side, boasted milk-white skin that, even under the harsh glare of the lights of the hospital room, looked pet-able. She had a little point to her chin that made her smile infectious, and her eyes were wide, the light brown almost hazel-gold. He had a feeling they changed with her mood. He loved eyes like that.

"I'm okay. Just moving around and trying to get more comfortable. The scaffolding didn't hurt me as much as I thought it did. Though if I hadn't moved when I did? Not sure."

"And you helped your sister. So, I guess a little pain's worth it?" Arden asked, her voice a little low.

"Bristol's smaller than I am. And if she had gotten hurt? I'd never have forgiven myself."

"But you're not the one who hurt her or yourself. You didn't sabotage the scaffolding, did you?"

"No, but I'm the big brother. My job is to protect her."

Arden rolled her eyes, and Liam raised his brows.

"Was that not the right answer? Am I just supposed to let her get hurt?"

"I'm not saying that. But you don't have to go all big brother overprotective caveman."

"Are we talking about me throwing myself on top of her body because the scaffolding fell? Or something else?"

Arden just shook her head and shrugged. When she did, she winced, and Liam wanted to reach out and help her. But he was in the same position as she was. A little too far away, and a bit too confined to the bed.

"I wasn't actually talking about you throwing yourself on her to protect her. That? That's a little heroic."

"Only a little?" he asked, teasing. He didn't want to think about the accident. Didn't want to think about what might have happened if something had hit Bristol. She *was* smaller, and for all Liam knew, it could have hit her in the head or been a lot worse than what happened to him.

"No, I'm talking about the fact that you said that she's your baby sister and, therefore, you have to protect her. It was all a little too familiar."

"Your brothers a little overprotective, are they?"

That could get in the way of things if he and Arden were to actually date.

Whoa. Where did that thought come from? He was just flirting with a pretty woman in the hospital, he wasn't actually thinking of dating her. Right?

"To say my brothers are overprotective would be an understatement. They think they always have reasons to be up in my business and treat me like I'm six. But I don't think their reasons are as good as they think they are." She looked down at her hands, and his gaze followed before returning to her face.

"Reasons?"

She shook her head. "Long story that I'm not really in the mood to get into. But, let's just say that my brothers are a bit territorial when it comes to me or anything I do or see or want to be near. So, if and when they show up again, I'm already sorry for the third degree they're going to give you."

That made Liam laugh. "So, you can't even sit in the same room with a guy without them getting all overprotective?"

"At this point, I don't even remember the last time I was in a room with a guy." Her eyes widened, and she put her hand over her mouth, her face going pale under her rash. "Forget I said that. Pretend I was all cool and knew exactly what I was saying."

"Want me to blame it on the drugs?" That made her laugh.

"Yes, let's do that."

The fact that she hadn't been in the same room with a guy for a while meant that she wasn't taken. Good to know. And was he thinking that he was going to ask her out? Maybe he should. Perhaps it had been far too long and being around someone who made him smile—even in their current state of things—was nice. It didn't have to be anything serious. He wasn't ready for that. Maybe not ever. But not being alone, even for a little bit, would be nice.

"Anyway, when do you think you're going to get out of here?" he asked, leaning back on the bed, trying to get a little more comfortable. His head hurt, and so did his arm, but he'd be fine. And it wasn't like his current job required a lot of heavy lifting or labor. In fact, it was only the fact that he hiked and used his home gym that he actually maintained the body that he'd had when he modeled.

He'd been a little slenderer when he was a model. He'd packed on muscle and some weight since then. Thank God.

He had never been into the twig thing. As he'd grown up, he'd widened a bit, mostly in his shoulders and his chest. But then he'd begun to get a few laugh lines on his face, and the modeling jobs had dried up. At least the ones that he had started in—fashion and other things.

So, he'd walked away. Now, he had a job where he could sit at a desk staring at a computer for fourteen hours a day if he weren't careful. Being a writer wasn't easy, and it really wasn't easy on his body. Thankfully, he actually liked his job. Usually.

Arden's voice once again pulled him out of his thoughts. "Hopefully, I'll be out soon. I really don't want them to keep me overnight, even if they were talking about admitting me."

Liam nodded. "Same. I guess it's a little busy today."

"Days when the sun is out, and people do stupid things tend to make the hospital a little busier than usual. Believe me."

His brows rose again. "Been in hospitals often, have you?" He'd only meant it as a tease, but when her face shut down, he cursed himself. "Sorry. Didn't mean to pry."

"No, it's okay. I've been in and out of hospitals a fair share of my time. And not just this one. You learn the ins and outs. But I'm fine." She said the last part quickly as if she were warding off any worry or pity. He didn't have pity. He was curious and hoped she was okay, but he wasn't going to pry. Not when she clearly didn't want him to.

"I haven't been in as many as some of my family members."

"Your brothers and sister are in and out of them?" Arden asked and then seemed to pull away. "And there I am, being curious about you when I kind of didn't want you to be about me."

"No worries. And I was actually talking about my cousins. They seem to be in and out of hospitals more often than not for one emergency or another. And that's not even counting births or normal checkups."

"Are they okay?"

"They are now. Just went through some things over the past few years. But that tends to happen when there are, like, twenty of them."

Arden's eyes widened, and she sat up ever so slightly without pulling on her IV. "Twenty? And they've all had to deal with emergencies like this?"

"Not that many, really. I promise. But if you add all the children, I think we're up to, like, a hundred family members at this point. It's a little ridiculous."

"Wow. I didn't even think that was possible."

"Well, one set of cousins makes up like eight of them. And then another set is four, and we're a set of four. And then there's a set of five. It adds up over time."

"That *is* a little ridiculous." He laughed at that.

"Tell me about it. Family reunions are a bitch."

"Where on Earth do you find the space for everybody?"

"One of my uncles down in Denver has a bunch of land that fits us all. So we hang out in the back yard, and sort of in their house too if it's rainy. It gets a little tight sometimes. But we make do. Actually, I don't really know if we can all fit now that everyone's starting to have kids."

"Do you have kids?"

"No. None of my siblings do. We're a little behind the times compared to the rest of the clan."

"Good to know."

He smiled then, and they continued talking about nothing important. Not about their jobs, or even about what ailed either of them. It was nice.

When the doctors came in to wheel Liam out for a test, he got Arden's number. He was surprised that she'd actually given it to him, but he was glad. Maybe he'd call her. He probably should, considering the hospital was a strange place to meet someone, but he didn't want to come off too needy. And considering that he felt that she had a few stories of her own, he really didn't want to push.

"It was nice to meet you, Arden," he said before they wheeled him out.

"It was good to see you, too, Liam."

"I'd make a line about having to fall or get hit in the head to see you, but I don't really know where to go with that without sounding like a weirdo."

That made her laugh, and she just shook her head. "Please don't hurt yourself trying to come up with one."

"Well, it's good that you've now seen me at my worst and still gave me your number."

"And it's good that you've seen me at one of my worst, and you asked."

He didn't pry into that cryptic statement, knowing there was definitely more beneath the words. But then again, there usually was more beneath the words.

Instead, he left without meeting her brothers—and,

thankfully, without his family coming at him from all sides.

The Montgomerys were a lot all at once. And from what Arden had said, her brothers were the same way. But he and Arden had had those moments together, and Liam figure it was a good thing. At least, he hoped it was.

BY THE TIME HE GOT HOME, LIAM WAS EXHAUSTED, AND all he wanted to do was sleep. His parents, his brothers, and his sister hadn't left him alone. In fact, the whole family had come to double check if he was okay and to see if he needed anything. Even Craig and Cain had stopped by on their way to their honeymoon, apologizing profusely for what had happened.

Liam didn't blame them. He just pushed them out gently, considering it was their honeymoon, and they deserved some time alone. They shouldn't be worrying about him. It wasn't their fault that the scaffolding on the building had fallen on him. It was the contractor's fault, and that was something maybe they would deal with later. Or not. He was fine. He had decent medical insurance, and his little sister hadn't been hurt. Nothing else mattered.

A full day had passed, and while he hurt, he had slept well thanks to a pain med or two. Of course, he wasn't actually alone in his house. It seemed like there was going to be a mini-family reunion in his damn living room. They had propped him up in his armchair with his feet up, and a glass of water by his side. He was pretty sure if he looked at all like he wanted anything, his mom or one of his siblings would be up getting it. He really didn't want that though, so he stayed silent and tried to keep his face blank.

His mom and dad were in the kitchen making dinner since, apparently, they were all eating at his house today.

Ethan had brought his best friend, Lincoln, and the two of them were talking about the game, even though he wasn't really paying attention. Bristol had shown up with her best friend, Marcus, and the two of them were talking books and completely ignoring Liam. Aaron sat on the couch right next to Liam, just glancing at him every once in a while but not talking.

The fact that everybody was at his house, and yet no one was actually talking to him was weird. Liam figured they all just wanted to make sure that he was okay and didn't really know *what* to do. His family wasn't the best at telling each other exactly what they were feeling or knowing how to help one another, so they tended to overreact and overprotect, much like Arden had said about her brothers.

Thinking about Arden made Liam remember the number in his phone. His lips quirked into a smile.

"So, what has you smiling like that?" Aaron asked, leaning back in his chair.

"Nothing."

"Could it be the girl in the bed next to you that I saw when I walked by yesterday?" Ethan asked and grinned.

Liam frowned. "Who?"

"Ah," Lincoln said, laughing. "Misdirection. You totally saw her." He turned to Ethan. "They were talking, weren't they?"

Ethan nodded and looked at his best friend. "Yep. They were talking. The conversation looked very much like flirting. Even though both of you guys were hooked up to IVs, you were still laughing."

"Oh? So, who is she? What does she do?"

Bristol leaned forward, and Marcus laughed, pulling her back onto the couch. "Leave your brother alone."

Bristol just narrowed her eyes at him and sank back into his hold. The two of them had been best friends for years and acted more like an old married couple than they did best friends. Liam was pretty sure they had never actually dated because Bristol couldn't keep a secret to save her life when it came to things like that. And he figured she'd have mentioned it to him, especially if they'd had too much to drink.

Liam might be the overprotective big brother like he had said to Arden, but he and Bristol told each other everything. They were Montgomerys. They were siblings. They were best friends. And they didn't fuck shit up with each other by keeping secrets.

"She's just a girl that I met."

"And?" Aaron asked.

"And she was sweet."

"Is she okay?" Bristol asked, sounding worried.

"She should be. At least, I think so. She told me she'd gotten too much sun and was getting treatment."

"Treatment?" Ethan asked. "Sounds like she's been dealing with something for a while if she used that word," he put in.

"I know. And I sort of broached the subject at one point, but she pulled away. I didn't think it was my business."

"At least, not yet," Bristol said. "But if you date her, it might become your business. You got her number, right?" Bristol smiled, and Liam rolled his eyes.

"You're an annoying little sister sometimes."

"I'm an annoying little sister all the time, according to you. And you totally got her number."

"Maybe."

"That's my man," Lincoln said, and Ethan punched his friend in the gut. "I cannot believe you just uttered that phrase."

"I can't either. Didn't sound like me." Lincoln grinned and then rubbed his stomach. "Stop hitting me. You have issues."

"*You* have issues."

Liam pinched the bridge of his nose and thought about maybe taking another pill so he could go to sleep. Perhaps he'd have a beer. He hadn't had a pain pill in long enough that he could probably have one. Beer and stitches were okay, right?

"Anyway, there's a couple of things for the hospital that you need to fill out," Ethan put in, going through them. "Apparently, they need your birth certificate for something. I don't really know why. I hate our healthcare system."

Liam frowned. "My birth certificate? Really? Shouldn't an insurance card work?"

"I don't know. They just said they needed a copy for something. I wasn't really paying attention. It's probably for insurance or something. Or whatever."

Liam tried to remember where he'd put his birth certificate. He was organized, truly, but he'd been on deadline, and his head hurt. "I think the original is in my lockbox up in my office. I don't actually have the copy that I used for school and stuff. I lost that in one of the moves like an idiot. But I have the original upstairs, I think."

"Okay, I'll get it. Got the keys?"

"On my ring. At least they were. They should be on the counter somewhere."

"Got it."

Liam just shook his head and rested while his siblings and their friends fought and laughed. His parents were still in the kitchen, making dinner and, knowing them, probably making out. They were still so in love, even after all this time. He didn't really understand how love could withstand the test of time, but his mom and dad were an excellent example of it.

"What do you think Mom and Dad are making for dinner tonight?" Bristol asked, looking down at her phone while Marcus peeked over her shoulder. They were probably looking up spoilers for their favorite TV show since they had missed an episode.

"I have no idea. But I think I'm finally getting hungry."

"That means you're getting better. That's good."

There was something in his sister's voice that made Liam pause. "What is it?"

"Nothing. Just...thank you."

Liam sighed. "You already thanked me. I did nothing special. You would have done the same thing."

"I know. All of us would have. But you still are the one who did it for me. So, I'll always be grateful."

"So am I," Marcus muttered. Liam frowned.

He didn't have time to think about that, though. Ethan was walking into the room, his face pale.

"What is it? Did you find it?"

Ethan nodded, his hands shaking where he held the paper.

"What? Is that not the right thing? Do I need to file for another one or something?" Liam tried to sit up and winced at the pain in his arm and then looked at Ethan.

"I found it. But...I don't think it's right."

Liam reached out for it. "What do you mean? It's just a birth certificate. It has my name, place of birth, maybe even my weight. Plus, it, you know, has Mom's and Dad's names and all of that. What could be wrong with it?"

Ethan met Liam's gaze, his eyes wide. "It...it has Mom's name. But... There's something wrong, Liam."

"Tell me."

The room went silent, and everyone stared. "What is it?"

"It doesn't have Dad's name. It doesn't say *Timothy Montgomery*. It has some guy named Steve on it. Who the fuck is Steve?"

At the sound of a shocked gasp behind Ethan, Liam turned. There was his mother, her face dead white, her hand over her mouth, and his father, Timothy Montgomery, looking as if they had seen a ghost.

Liam blinked, staring at the man who had his chin, his build, and his eyes...and wondered what the hell had just happened.

CHAPTER 4

"*L*iam," his mother began. He held up a hand, needing to collect his thoughts. He didn't want to have this conversation. Didn't want whatever she obviously had to say to come out of her mouth.

He swore he could hear everyone breathing as one. Could hear their rapid heartbeats as they all tried to calm themselves so they could figure out what to say and what to do. Or figure out what should be said at all.

Liam turned his head away from his parents, needing to focus on something else so he wouldn't say something he'd regret later. Instead, he looked at his brothers, his sister, and wondered what he could say to make this better for them.

He was the big brother, the one who fixed things. But he was so damn afraid that he wouldn't be able to fix this.

Bristol looked over at him, her blue eyes wide, her dark hair pulled back from her face. He let out a breath, then turned to Aaron, his brother's blue eyes narrowed as his jaw tightened, his dark hair messy around his face for the first time in a long while. Then Liam turned to Ethan and looked at his blue eyes, dark hair, and strong jaw.

All blue eyes. Yet Liam had hazel ones.

Just like his mother's family.

Or so he thought. So he'd been told.

Jesus Christ.

"Liam," his father began. Liam looked up, wondering what this man could possibly say, what the hell was going on. Because there was no way anything could be said at that moment to make things better. Not one single fucking thing.

"I need a minute." Liam put down the footrest of his chair and stood up, wincing at the pain in his arm and in his head. He was fine. He hadn't been hurt too badly. But now it felt like he'd been knocked for a loop, confused as all hell regarding what was going on.

"Let me see that," Liam said, putting his hand out to Ethan. His brother hesitated. "Hand over the damn paper, Ethan."

Ethan met his gaze, and his face paled as he handed over the birth certificate. Both of their parents reached out as if they wanted to stop him.

But there was no stopping this.

"I...the fuck?" he whispered to himself, looking down at the paper in his hands.

Steve Stark.

Who the hell was Steve Stark, and why was he on Liam's birth certificate? Why hadn't he seen this before? Was this just a mistake? Liam looked up at his mother's tear-filled eyes and then at the strong line of tension in his father's jaw and had a feeling it wasn't a mistake.

But a mistake had been made. Many of them.

This just wasn't one of them.

"What am I looking at here?" Liam asked, his voice surprisingly steady. See? He wasn't going to blow his lid and burn the house down. Though he damn well wanted to.

Bristol was suddenly standing by him, her hand on his back as she rubbed small circles. He couldn't feel it, not really. He couldn't feel much of anything. This had just been blown out of proportion. Or wasn't anything. It had to be.

Marcus stood by Bristol's side, and Liam had a feeling the other man, as well as Lincoln, probably wanted to leave. But they didn't. They were family, too—at least that's what Liam's parents said over and over again. They were family.

Then what the fuck did that make Liam?

"Who the fuck is Steve Stark?" Liam asked, ignoring the way Aaron and Ethan moved closer to him.

They were either all trying to be strong for him, or were just as confused as he was. He didn't know which. But he needed fucking answers.

"Maybe we should all sit down?" Timothy Montgomery said, his voice low, steady. Way too steady.

"Maybe you should tell me what I'm looking at first and *then* we'll sit down. Then you're going to tell me what the hell is going on. Because this has to be a mistake, right? Ethan got the wrong piece of paper, or there was just an error. But with the way Mom is crying, and how you look so fucking pale? Yeah, I'm going to need some answers."

"Liam," Aaron said, his voice low.

"No, you don't get to be the calm and steady one. Not right now," Liam said to his brother, narrowing his eyes. He wasn't angry at Aaron, wasn't mad at any of his siblings. But then again... Were they really his siblings? Jesus Christ. His chest tightened, and he fought to keep breathing. Fought to keep thinking.

"I think we should go," Lincoln whispered, and Liam looked out of the corner of his eye as Marcus gave the other man a tight nod. The two of them left, leaving just the Montgomerys in the house.

It was quiet as they closed the door behind the men, and Liam wondered what the hell anyone could say to make things better. That was usually his job, making things better, even if Aaron was generally the cool and collected one. Ethan was the one that always seemed as if he had things figured out, even if he was sometimes the funnier one. Bristol tied them all together and cared for them all.

But Liam couldn't really make sense of anything just then. Couldn't focus.

"Okay, we're going to do this," Timothy said, letting out a breath. "Before you were born, your mother and I had been dating for a while."

Liam looked up, wanting to tell Timothy to stop. He wanted to tell his father to stop. He didn't want to hear the words. Didn't want to look down at the piece of paper that was now crumpled in one fist. He didn't want any of this. But there was no turning back from the secrets. No turning away from the things that would hurt. He had learned that long ago. His whole family had.

And now, he couldn't run away. Couldn't walk out the door like Lincoln and Marcus had done.

They had the option to leave because they weren't blood.

Though now Liam was afraid that he could just walk away, too. Because maybe he didn't have that connection at all.

"We'd been dating for a while, and while we loved each other, we fought. A lot."

Timothy reached out and grabbed Francine's hand, giving it a squeeze. Liam just stood there, blinking.

None of the siblings spoke. It was as if they were waiting for Liam to react first, or they just wanted the story.

He didn't know. Wasn't sure he cared. All he could do was try to listen through the pounding in his ears. Try to breathe through the fact that it felt like his stomach was about to revolt. Maybe he should have eaten something with his final pain med. Perhaps he should just leave.

"We loved each other, but we were young. Sometimes, when you're young, you do stupid things."

"We broke up," Francine said, raising her chin. "We had actually broken up. We weren't *on a break* like anything Ross did with Rachel."

Liam watched as Francine met Bristol's gaze. His mother smiled, though it didn't reach her eyes. Liam didn't know if his sister smiled back, but he knew the two had a connection, and Francine wanted that comfort.

But Liam didn't care. Not yet.

Maybe not ever.

"Your father and I had been broken up for a few weeks. It felt like it had been the day before, and yet it felt like months. It just hurt. I didn't know how much I loved him until I didn't have him anymore. So, my friend and I went out, and I got drunk. I decided to drink my worries away, and I had too much fun."

Francine let out a hiccuping sob and then straightened her shoulders, looking like someone Liam had never met before. "I slept with someone else. Only once. But one night was enough. We were safe, but I got pregnant. And then, the next month, your father and I got back together. We were back together for about a month when I realized that I was pregnant with you. And because of how things stood, we knew it couldn't be your father's."

Liam just blinked, trying to process everything that had just been said. "You had a one-night stand when you got drunk and slept with some man named Steve? And you still married Dad?" He said the word *Dad*, but it didn't feel right. And he could tell the others felt the same way because both of his parents flinched.

But they weren't his parents, were they? Well, his mom was, but his dad couldn't be. At least, not by blood. What the fuck? He couldn't focus.

"We got married after you were born, something you've always known."

Liam gave a tight nod. "Yeah, I knew that I was born before marriage, that's nothing new to me."

"Your dad and I had a lot of issues while I was pregnant, trying to come to terms with what we were going to do, and how we were going to be with each other. And because of that, and because we didn't really know what was right or wrong, we put Steve's name on the birth certificate."

"So, this man Steve Stark is my father?"

"No, this man at my side is your father. He's the one who raised you. He has been your dad your entire life, Liam. That doesn't change. A name on a line, someone I only saw twice in my life, doesn't change that."

Liam straightened. "Twice?"

His mother raised her chin again, her eyes dry. "I found him again so I could get him to sign over parental rights. He had his own plans, and I wasn't part of them. I didn't want to be part of them. When your father and I got married—"

"You mean Timothy," Liam cut in, his voice sharp.

"Liam," Bristol whispered.

Liam looked down at his little sister and shook his head. "No, not now."

He pinched the bridge of his nose, tried to collect his thoughts. He couldn't breathe, couldn't think like he knew he should. Jesus.

"So, let me get this straight. You slept with another man, got pregnant, and while you and this guy,"—he pointed at Timothy—"were trying to figure out exactly what you were going to do, I ended up with some other man's name on my birth certificate. The one I have right here." He shook the piece of paper in the air. "So, why the hell was Timothy's name on my birth certificate? I mean, the one that I've been using this whole time."

"Because I adopted you," Timothy snapped. "Your mom and I got married, Steve signed over his rights, and

I adopted you. And in the state of Colorado, you can get that changed on the birth certificate, especially within the first year. I am your father. I was the one who raised you. Your mother and me. I have always been your dad. You are Liam Montgomery. You're not that guy, Steve's."

"No, because he didn't want me, did he? Instead? You've all been lying to me. For how long? I'm thirty-five fucking years old, you guys. You didn't think that maybe I might need to know this at some point in my life? What if I had done one of those AncestryDNA kits that are all the rage right now? What if I had figured something out on my own? Why the hell did I have to figure it out this way?"

"Liam, it's not what you think. We have always been your parents."

"That's not really the truth, is it?" Liam took a step back, the hollowness in his chest expanding as he tried to fight for breath. Bristol grabbed his hand, and Ethan and Aaron each put their hands on his shoulders, but he pushed them away, needing to be alone. Needing to think.

"Don't talk to your mother like that," Timothy said, and Liam shook his head. "You guys need to leave."

"No, we're going to talk about this." His father raised his voice and glared. "Yes, we should have found a way to tell you what happened, but we didn't. That's on us. But, like you said, we've had thirty-five fucking years with you. I'm your father. I was there when you said your first word. *Dad*, by the way. I was there when you took your first steps. I taught you how to ride a fucking bike. I was there to take you to your first job. I helped you learn how to drive. I have always been there. Your mother has always been there. We're your parents. Not some guy whose name was on your birth certificate for a month of your life."

"I need you to go," Liam whispered, his voice hollow. His hands shook, and he just looked down at the piece of paper in his fist, the one that said the wrong name but was actually the right one.

Despite that, he was a Montgomery. At least, that's what he had always thought.

The Montgomerys stayed together, were there for each other, no matter what. They each had a tattoo with the family's crest, for God's sake. An M and an I for Montgomery Ink and the Montgomery iris. It was the design that every single Montgomery had somewhere on them. His was on his arm, combined with the rest of his sleeve, and yet...was it even real? Was he a fucking Montgomery at all?

"Go," Liam whispered. "Just, go."

"We're going to talk about this," his father said. "We're going to give you time, but we're going to talk about this. Because you're my son. No matter what you're thinking right now, you are my goddamn son."

His mother reached out, but Liam took a step back, afraid of what he might say if she touched him. He didn't hate her. He didn't hate anyone. But he couldn't think.

He knew that step back was the wrong thing to do when he saw the pain on his mother's face, and the confusion on his father's. But they left him anyway. Walked out and left him to his thoughts, and with his siblings.

"Liam, it doesn't mean anything," Bristol said quickly. "You're still our brother. It's just a name, like you said. It means nothing. Dad has always been there for us."

"*Your* dad," Liam grumbled, knowing he was an idiot and that he was saying all the wrong things. He knew what being a father truly meant. It wasn't just the blood in your veins. But he couldn't focus on that right now. He couldn't concentrate on anything.

"You guys need to go, too," Liam barked.

"If you think we're going to fucking leave you alone right now, you've got to be crazy," Ethan snapped. "Yeah, I'd be pissed off, too. I *am* pissed off. They lied to all of us our entire lives. But you're still my fucking brother."

"You'll always be our brother," Aaron added.

"But I'm not a fucking Montgomery, am I?" Liam growled, throwing his hands up into the air. He winced at the movement that stretched the stitches on his arm, and then he cursed.

"Just go. I need time to think."

"If you take too much time, you're going to take the wrong next steps, and you're going to do something stupid," Bristol said quickly, tears running down her cheeks.

"Thanks for that vote of confidence," Liam said snidely. "I just need a minute to think."

"Then think with us," Aaron said softly. "Nothing's changed. You're still our brother. Can't you see that?"

"Am I? Why did they lie to us all this time if it didn't mean anything? I...I don't know what to think, but the lies...I don't know if I can handle that. I just need some time to think. I need you guys to go. Okay? I just need time to think." He said it aloud, but also kept repeating that in his head, over and over again. But he couldn't get his thoughts together.

How was he supposed to think when he had no idea what was going on? He'd always known that he had been born a bastard, at least in the sense of being born before his parents were married, but he hadn't known the whys of it. It had never bothered him that his birthday was before his parents' anniversary. It hadn't meant anything to him.

But now, it meant everything. And he couldn't figure out exactly why.

He looked down at his arm, at the MI tattoo that shone brightly amongst the flowers and other images on his skin. And he wondered what the hell he was going to do.

"You'll always be our brother," Bristol said through tears. "No matter what."

Liam looked up and shook his head. "Maybe. But if I'm not a Montgomery, what am I?"

No one could answer that. He didn't think there *was* an answer at all.

Because everyone had lied to him from the beginning. And if there was one thing he couldn't handle, it was lies. And now?

Now, he had nothing.

Not even his name.

CHAPTER 5

*a*rden didn't want to whine, but then again, she really did. Maybe because her eyes were crossing, and though her body felt better than it had last week, she still wanted to curl up into a ball and cry. The phrase, "Oh, God, everything hurts, and I'm dying," had been uttered a few times that day.

Mostly aloud. The rest just in her mind.

That's what happened when she worked by herself in her own home and rarely talked to people. Yes, she had a decent group of friends online, but she never actually saw them in person. And despite what her brothers thought, her online friends were her true friends. Just because she didn't see them every day—or *any* day since they lived all over the country—and didn't have coffee with them, didn't mean they weren't actual friends.

If she kept telling herself that, maybe she'd actually believe it when she needed to fight with her brothers about it.

The thing was, she didn't have as many friends as some might want her to have. She worked alone from her house, and that meant she didn't really have a lot of social interaction beyond her brothers and what happened online. She was relatively closed off from the world, and most days when she wasn't feeling her best, and the lupus and everything that came with it was hitting her hard, she was fine with that. Other days? She really missed human interaction.

Arden rolled her neck, looked down at her work, and smiled. Later today, she would have some human interaction.

Maybe it wasn't a date with the hot guy from the hospital, but that was fine. It wasn't like she believed that Liam Montgomery was going to ask her out. Because hot guys really didn't ask her out or follow through, even after getting her number.

She remembered how she'd looked that day and the fact that she'd had slight sunstroke and an allergic reaction that had led right to a lupus attack.

She was surprised that Liam had even wanted to speak with her. He'd probably just asked for her number out of pity.

She ignored the roiling in her stomach and went back

to work. She had things to do today that weren't just looking at words, and she would get to them.

Then she'd have her small interaction with humans and could get back to just hanging out with her dog.

As if he had known that she was thinking of him, Jasper put his head on her lap and looked up at her with those big, sad eyes of his. They had just gotten back from a walk less than an hour ago, so she knew it wasn't that. He probably just knew that she wasn't feeling her best and wanted to cuddle her.

"I love you, too, my little baby Jasper." She kissed the top of his head, and he rumbled a bit before going back to nap at her feet.

Jasper was a white Siberian Husky and possibly the cutest dog in the history of the world—at least in her opinion. He was getting older now, and not as quick as he once was, but he was still faster than she was. Thankfully, he wasn't a puppy anymore, and that meant that he rested more so she could, as well. When he was a puppy?

Yeah, that really hadn't gone over well with her lupus. Not even a little.

But she'd dealt with it, and she would deal with more later. She always did.

Right now, she had to get back to work.

She was the owner and sole proprietor of Literally Addictive Research. That sounded much more boring than it actually was.

She did research and book compendiums for sci-fi and historical fiction. Even though her personal love for reading was romance and young adult, she tended not to work in those two genres much. Mostly because she didn't want to deal with trying to organize facts and data and think about if the author and editor had actually researched anything while she was enjoying it.

In her line of work, she couldn't just relax while reading a book. So, she tried not to work in her preferred genres. Instead, she worked in two that she liked but didn't read for pleasure as often.

At the moment, she was reading a massive sci-fi series that she had been working on for seven books. She was now on the eighth. It was apparently the penultimate book, but she could tell that there could possibly be a spinoff series from the way certain side characters had been introduced.

She was happy for that because the author was brilliant with their prose, and their world building was phenomenal. But the author hated making their own series bible—or book compendium as they liked to call them. And that meant that Arden was going through every minute detail and double-checking the compendium that she had made for earlier books, making sure the facts were correct. Plus, she had to add every side character and what happened to those characters along the timeline to her work. It not only helped the author and the editor, but it also helped her enjoy the book a bit more.

At times, it got a little tedious, but her love of spread-sheets and data, as well as creative fiction, really melded together perfectly for this job.

Plus, there were a few key things for the next book that the client wanted her to research, but she needed to make sure she got this book done first. Because even though they were making up fake space ships and other things that didn't exist yet in the real world, their propulsion systems were based on true science. At least, somewhat. So, that meant that it was Arden's responsibility to make sure that everything made sense. No, her job wasn't the easiest, but it was perfect for her. Plus, her next project was for L.M. Berry, her favorite historical fiction and thriller author.

She could work from home and do things right from her bed if the rest of her body wasn't cooperating.

Thankfully, even though she was a little weaker than she wanted to be, she wasn't in a full-blown attack. Flareups were a bitch, and even though her body was sometimes in a constant state of flux, this one wasn't that bad.

Her hair didn't hurt too much, and her skin didn't feel like it was on fire.

Thankfully, the rash that Liam had seen was now completely gone, though she knew it might come back any day now because there was sun outside. But she was doing okay.

And okay was better than nothing.

Arden finished up the rest of her work—at least to a stopping point because she knew the work never truly ended. She wasn't going to complain about that, though, because work meant income and an actual job. She was so grateful that she got to do what she loved for a living and do it from her home in leggings and a comfortable shirt. But still, sometimes, she just needed to rest her eyes.

Lupus wasn't good for her eyeballs, after all. So, she wore reading glasses with a very low prescription and a blue-light lens just so she could focus for long periods of time.

She seriously had issues. But then, didn't everyone? She put her things away and got off her comfy chair with Jasper at her side. The soft sounds of his claws clicking against her hardwood floor made her smile, then reminded her that he probably needed to go to the groomer soon.

Most Siberian Huskies didn't really need to go to the groomers, but Jasper liked it, and sometimes, Arden was a little too weak to brush him for long periods of time. Her baby was a diva, and she loved it.

Arden turned on an audiobook for one of her favorite young adult fantasy romances and turned up the speed so she could listen at a comfortable pace as she started her next piece of work.

She didn't actually get paid to bake, but she loved it. Today, she was trying out a new recipe. A butterscotch brownie with white chocolate chips. It was from one of the contestants on a British baking show that she loved to watch. Their cookbook had just come out, and since it was their first one, she was going to try a new recipe. She had purchased around ten or eleven cookbooks from the show over the years, but she constantly bought more.

Baking soothed her. Plus, she loved eating all the goodies. Not that she was going to eat many of them today.

No, today was for the senior center.

See? She did talk with other people. And not just those online. She was going to do some baking, and even though it had sugar in it, some of those at the senior center would be grateful, including the nurses and staff who worked there.

Then she would take some pictures and put her final results up on the blog.

Yes, she had a food blog. Though it wasn't a huge one with an immense following, it helped her connect with the outside world.

Since this wasn't her recipe, she was going to help the actual author by mentioning the book and her results.

She liked doing a mixture of her own stuff and recipes she found.

It seemed to drive up viewings, and the ad revenue from the site helped her pay her medical bills.

She had many talents, but leaving the house sometimes wasn't one of them.

She danced around her kitchen—or at least she tried to dance. She wasn't the best at it, but she enjoyed herself. All the while, she listened to her book, tried to keep her dog out of her baking, and used a little bit of her energy to enjoy herself.

Sometimes, she felt cut off from the world. Other times, she was okay.

She had enough human interaction in her life. She didn't need men like Liam Montgomery getting her hopes up.

She didn't need anyone. She had herself.

Jasper nudged her, and she looked down at her Siberian Husky. "I need you, too, my baby boy."

He seemed to smile at her and then trotted out of the room, most likely to find a place to nap since he wasn't getting any of her baked goods.

It took a few hours, but soon, the brownies were baked, mostly cooled, and in a container so she could take them to the senior center. She checked the clock and was grateful that she'd woken up before the crack of dawn so her day started early enough that she could do everything that she wanted to and still rest. She quickly changed into some cute jeans and a top that didn't look like she'd slept in it. There wasn't much she could do with her hair today, but a cute bun that was actually brushed counted for something.

Then she pulled on a light jacket, stuffed her feet into some cute boots, and grabbed her baked goods.

"Sorry, Jasper, I'll come home to you soon, and then we'll go for a W-A-L-K."

His eyes brightened at that comment, and she held back a wince. Apparently, the way she'd spelled it meant that he actually knew what the word meant. She'd have to find a new word that meant the same thing. Much like when she had been younger, and her family had stopped using the word *snack*, and started to use the word *treat*, and then had to spell out the words. Either way, their dog had always known when it was time for something good to eat.

Dogs were much smarter than people gave them credit for.

Arden let her Bluetooth in her car work and continued listening to her book as she headed towards the senior center.

Sandy, the woman in charge of the center, or at least in charge of welcoming her, smiled as Arden walked in. "Oh, good. I remember you said you were going to stop by, but I'm glad you did."

Arden didn't take offense to that statement. Sometimes, even though she really wanted to come, her body wouldn't let her. And the people working here, they truly understood why Arden sometimes didn't show up. Oh, yes, she called and came by as soon as she could with baked goods. But she hated letting people down. Therefore, having a job and other things where she could work from home or keep those who relied on her to a minimum was good for her.

She might be a few decades younger than the people who lived in the center, but a couple of them had her same disease, and sometimes, she felt like she was their age.

But today was a good day, at least mostly, and she was going to stop thinking about that.

"So, I have a new recipe. It has butterscotch in it."

"George is going to love that. You know him and his butterscotch sweet tooth."

Arden smiled and handed over the container. "Oh, I do. Plus, a little birdie told me you like butterscotch, too."

Sandy beamed. "I will have one tiny brownie. I'm not allowed to have another." She tapped her hip, and Arden just smiled. Sandy was in her forties, looked like she was at least a decade younger, and was very fit. It was hard work at the center. Plus, she knew that Sandy did as many half marathons and 5Ks as she could.

Arden had never even tried to do one of those. She

only ran if she thought a zombie might be chasing her. Oh, she ran if she was walking Jasper, and he got a little too excited, but that wasn't that often. Jasper was a good boy and liked to take care of her. Dragging her around and forcing her to run was not a way to do that.

"You look amazing."

"And you are wonderful to say that. Now, let's dig into these, and you can say hello to the few people in the TV and craft rooms."

"As long as I'm not interrupting anything," Arden said quickly.

"You aren't. George and the others will love to see you."

"I'll be glad to see them, too."

About eighty percent of this particular senior center's occupants had no family members. That wasn't always the case, but right now, there were a lot of lonely people at the center, and if Arden could help at least a bit just by being there, that was good.

It was one of her worst fears to one day be in a center like this without anyone visiting her.

She pushed that thought away, thinking it ridiculous. She had four overprotective brothers that were always there for her. There was no way she would end up like this. Even if she one day found herself not being able to live on her own because her illness got the best of her, she'd have a place to go.

She would always have someone to rely on.

She just wished she could be someone they could rely on, too. And…that was enough of that.

"Okay, darling, I see you brought me something sweet to eat," George said, his bushy brows waggling as he laughed with her.

"You're allowed to have one. You know the rules." Arden did her best to sound prim and proper as she sat next to the older man and waved at the others as they looked up from their books or their chess games or from the TV.

Everyone knew her here, and it felt like another home. She liked it, even though her energy was lagging just a bit from her long day.

"When are you going to bring a nice man for us to meet?" Samantha said as she came to sit next to them. Samantha was in her seventies and could probably run a half marathon if she wanted. Arden seriously had no idea how the other woman did it.

"I've brought all of my brothers here before."

"Brothers, ha!" Samantha flipped her hand in the air. "Not that I don't admire the eye candy," Samantha said, laughing.

"I don't think so," Arden said, holding up her hands. "Never use the phrase *eye candy* when you're talking about my brothers. Please."

"I don't know, Arden, they are some nice hunks of meat," George said, laughing.

"I have no idea if hunks of meat is a real phrase, but we're just never going to repeat it. As for bringing a nice young man? I have George right here. What other man do I need?" Arden said.

Samantha met George's gaze, and then they both looked at Arden. She held up her hands in protest again before reaching down for the tray of brownies. "How about we just eat brownies and never talk about this again?"

"For now," Samantha said, picking up a sweet treat. "For now."

And at that ominous tone, Arden just shook her head and promptly changed the subject to the latest gossip.

She stayed for an hour, all of their energy seeming to lag ever so slightly as time passed, and then took her now-empty container back to her car after saying goodbye.

This time, she turned on the radio because she couldn't really focus on her book as much as she wanted to and made her way home.

Jasper was waiting for her, his doggy smile bright and happy when he saw her. She went down to her knees and hugged him tightly, knowing that she needed to muster up the energy to take him for a walk.

She wasn't dying. She was fine. She just hated that

some days she didn't have enough spoons. She didn't have the energy to do all the things she wanted to do, and she hated herself for it sometimes.

But before she could berate herself any more, the door opened behind her. She looked over her shoulder and narrowed her eyes.

"You're not going to knock anymore, are you?" she asked as her brothers walked through the door, their arms laden with groceries.

She was both annoyed and relieved to see them. Tears filled her eyes, and she quickly blinked them away before anyone saw them.

But, from the way Cross looked at her, she knew she hadn't been fast enough.

No, her brothers knew exactly what she needed, even if she didn't want to need it.

"We brought groceries. And tonight, we're doing a family dinner at your house." Cross looked at her then, his arms folded over his chest. "And you don't get to complain about it."

Arden stood quickly and then wrapped her arms around his waist. When she rested her head on his chest, he moved his arms out of the way and hugged her tightly.

"Thank you," she whispered.

"Always, little sister," Cross said, kissing the top of her head.

"Okay, it's time for a walk," Prior said, and Jasper danced around him.

Arden smiled as Prior hooked the leash onto Jasper's collar, and then the two of them were off, Macon trailing them as the three decided it was time for a run rather than a walk. That would be good because Jasper could work out the last of his energy, and they would be able to sleep well tonight.

"Now, I was thinking lasagna for dinner," Nate said. "What do you think?"

"Well, did you buy everything for lasagna?" Arden asked, hugging her brother's waist.

"Of course."

"Did you want me to make the lasagna?" Arden asked, knowing where this was going. Her brothers could all cook, but she was the best at it. And they loved her lasagna.

"I am going to let you cook if you want, but I will be your sous chef. Meaning, I will do all the heavy lifting, and I will force you onto a chair if I have to if you get too tired. And, yes, I realize the irony of us coming over with groceries and forcing you to cook us dinner. But, dear God, we were talking about lasagna and garlic bread the entire time we were grocery shopping, and I think my mouth is still watering."

Cross let out a rough chuckle behind her, and she smiled. See? She could be relied on. She could be needed.

She didn't need anything else.

She had her brothers, she was about to have some amazing food, she had her work life, her online life, and friends that may not be her age but knew her and loved her.

She had more than she needed.

She didn't need a phone call from the hot, tattooed guy from the hospital.

She just needed herself and everything she already had.

CHAPTER 6

*A*rden set down her book and grinned. L.M. Berry was seriously one of the best authors of all time, and this book might be her favorite. Yes, she did the book bible for it, as well as helped with some of the research for the author, but being able to sit down and read it for fun as well took it to a whole other level.

With L.M. Berry in particular, she didn't actually read the book until after it was published or at least ready for publication to add to her bible. Thankfully, the author seemed to use the compendium she had been working on for the past few years well enough that she hadn't found any mistakes when it came to inconsistencies that she might have caught during an earlier reading. Either that or his editors and copy editors were on their game. It was probably a combination of everything, though she figured there would probably be a mistake eventually. There always was. And readers found them. But it was her job to help.

However, today, she was just reading for fun. She had been baking all morning and then did a little work, so now she just wanted to relax.

She was trying to go slow and savor the book rather than finish it in a day like she could do. She wanted to enjoy it. Though going slow wasn't the easiest thing to do when it came to this series.

She couldn't help it. She loved reading about Nash, the protagonist, who fought against the enemy, recovered lost artifacts, and dove into the world of real-life historical heroes.

It was a little Indiana Jones, a bit of history, and a whole lot of fun.

Plus, it seemed that the author had decided to finally add in a love interest for Nash. And since romance was Arden's favorite genre, this woman named Penny just made her smile.

She really hoped that Penny didn't die in the end like so many other books that Arden had read that weren't romances.

Seriously, how hard was it to just let someone have a happily ever after?

She let out a sigh and then got up from the couch, stretching her back as she did. Happily ever after?

Considering that she hadn't found one herself, maybe it was only right that this book didn't either. After all, it was sometimes hard to believe in them outside of stories when a guy didn't even call you after he'd asked for your number.

But that was enough of that. Seriously, just because it had been over two weeks since she'd had her flareup and met Liam Montgomery, didn't mean it was the end of the world. She had been through so much, things much worse than having a man not call her. It wasn't even worth stressing about.

Arden set the book on her coffee table, making sure it was out of the way of Jasper's tail. Sometimes, he got a little happy and knocked things off surfaces. It wasn't his fault, there were things in his way.

Yes, her brothers called her an animal apologist, but she wasn't sorry. Even the irony of that statement made her smile.

It wasn't Jasper's fault that he had been the most adorable little puppy ever and just happened to be a big puppy now that needed things a certain way. If they were in his way, they tended to get knocked to the floor. She just had to work with that.

"And I love you all the more for it," she sing-songed to her dog as she bent down to kiss the top of his head.

She winced, looking down at him as she shook her

CARRIE ANN RYAN

head. "Seriously, I can't believe I can't get that out of your fur."

He gave her a big doggy smile, his white fur no longer completely pristine but a beautiful shade of blue.

She had been baking cupcakes earlier that morning for one of the community centers near her home. She'd even dropped them off earlier before coming back to read her book.

She was very grateful that she had made extra frosting. Because a certain perfect little puppy hadn't been so perfect. He had gotten into the blue frosting. Thankfully, everything she used was all-natural, but his beautiful white fur was now just a touch blue.

She couldn't help that she had been making unicorn cupcakes complete with horns.

Their beautiful blue-frosted peaks had been the sky, and Jasper had apparently really liked the frosting.

"You're a menace, my little blue cookie and cupcake monster." Jasper danced around her, and she laughed.

Her whole body felt better that day. It had for the past three days, in fact. Because of that, it seemed that Jasper was feeling better, too. Her dog tended to have the same moods that she did. So, if she wasn't feeling well, he was a little more solemn and would press his body to hers as if he knew she needed the heat and the comfort.

But when she was feeling good and able to dance around the house and actually get things done, he was

80

like his old puppy self, running around and even sometimes being a bit ornery. He was a very well-behaved dog, so sometimes he was allowed to be a little dorky.

He was her dog, after all.

Being a dork was sort of part of the requirements.

"Do you want to go for a walk?" she asked, raising her voice at the end so Jasper's ears perked up. He didn't disappoint her and then danced around her again before sitting perfectly still and raising one paw like a gentleman.

"You're such a good boy. Yes, you are." She shook his paw, patted his head, and then went to get his leash.

She slid her feet into her new loafers that she was completely in love with that were comfortable to walk in and cute enough that she wouldn't look like a bag lady if she ran into any of her neighbors. One too many times of having dirty hair covered in dry shampoo, wearing a baggy shirt with crumbs on it, and leggings that probably had a few more holes than she would have liked, was enough for her. Her neighbors probably already thought she was the weird hermit who never left the house other than to walk her dog. She even got her groceries delivered most weeks because, sometimes, her body just wasn't feeling it.

It wasn't that she was lazy, it was that she had things to do and limited energy to do them. And, sometimes, her body didn't let her do all the things she wanted. All the conveniences like Prime shipping and delivery services for stuff like groceries and even her wine meant that she didn't have to waste her energy—what little of it she sometimes had—on dealing with other humans.

She left the house. She had just been at the community center that morning for an hour after all. Hadn't she?

"Today, it's all about you, my favorite boy," she sang to her dog as he pranced next to her. As soon as she opened the door, though, he quit with the prancing. He lifted his head and regally strode down the sidewalk with her trailing behind him after she had closed the door.

He might act like a dork just for her, but she swore he changed the way he moved whenever he was outside so others knew what a glorious beast he was.

Even if his face was stained blue.

Because, of course, he was her dog.

They walked their mile circuit, one that she did as many times a day as she could.

She could walk for longer, but she never wanted to push herself just in case she had a flareup in the middle of her walk. So, she did her single mile—something that Jasper didn't mind—though she tried to do it multiple times a day.

They were about at the half-mile mark when Jasper pulled at his leash.

"Jasper, behave."

But then she knew it was a lost cause. A rabbit darted out from behind a bush, and another chased after it.

Because Jasper was in a playful mood that day, he followed.

When she tried to pull him back, her hand suddenly gave out, her body weakening just enough that she couldn't hold him.

"Jasper!" she shouted, chasing after him.

The thing was, her dog was *fast*.

Much faster than she was. She quickly chased after him, turning the corner as her feet pounded against the pavement, grateful that she was wearing comfortable shoes but kind of wishing she had put on her tennis shoes. She hadn't realized that she'd be running after her dog, though.

He never chased rabbits, at least outside of her yard. And he always listened to her. Today was not their day, apparently.

He was not getting a treat later. But, damn it, what if he got hit by a car? What if someone found him and took him? What if he got hurt? She would never forgive herself if he got hurt because she hadn't been strong enough to hold him. He was a large dog, and a big responsibility. She had to be better.

As soon as she turned the corner again, her heart beating fast, and her mouth going dry, she almost tripped over herself when she found Jasper calmly sitting at the feet of a very tall man. His tail bounced, his big doggy smile wide as he looked at her over his shoulder.

The dog. Not the man. The man did not have a doggy smile. No, he had a smirk. A large one that made her insides do funny things. It made her wonder why fate was so cruel.

She knew her face was red once again, and her hair was likely sticking to the sweat on her forehead. She hadn't been wearing the right bra for a jog, so she had a feeling she wasn't all the way situated in her shirt correctly.

She wanted to grip her side, wondering why her whole body hurt from just a slight run in the wrong shoes.

But Jasper was okay, and...he wasn't alone.

"Liam," she gasped out, sucking in a breath. "That's... that's my dog. Jasper. Get over here." She did her best to make herself sound stern, and Jasper lowered his head, looking sad.

She would not give in to that face. Not to the cute, blue spots on his white fur, or his big, sad eyes.

"You were a bad dog. Come here."

She held out her hand, and Liam took a few steps forward before handing over the leash.

"Sorry. I caught him, but I didn't mean to get him in trouble."

"No, I'm sorry," she whispered with a wince. "The

tone of voice was for my dog. I thought he would come to me. I didn't really realize you'd have to hand over the leash. I'm not thinking clearly. I was just so scared."

She looked down at Jasper. "Do you hear me? I was worried. You don't run off like that. Never do that again." Then she went down to her knees and hugged Jasper tightly. He put his big paw on her shoulder, and she nuzzled into him.

"Don't scare me like that."

She knew she probably looked a little bit insane, holding her dog as he hugged her back. But he was one of the only people in her life, and he wasn't even a person.

Most everyone else had left her over time. Partly because they couldn't stand by as their lives kept moving forward, and hers kept getting stuck in the past. It took a lot of energy to be sick, to keep living when everything kept pulling at you. Some people had lives of their own and needed to continue living. And they had to stop waiting for those who had to struggle just a little bit more.

Arden stood up, aware that her entire body was likely covered in dog hair at this point.

"It's okay," Liam said. "Here, let me help you up." He held out his palm, and Arden blinked before reaching out and putting her free hand into his, keeping her other hand firmly on Jasper's leash.

"So...hi." She wasn't very good at this whole thing. Whatever *this* was.

Liam let go of her hand and stuffed his into his pocket, rocking back on his heels as he studied the two of them. Arden couldn't help but notice the way his hair fell across his forehead and how his grin quirked at the corner of his mouth.

He was just as handsome as he had been in the hospital. All hard lines, yet with a softness about him that came from humor. Or at least that's what she thought. Maybe she was just looking too hard into it. After all, he hadn't called her. Hadn't texted.

She didn't know why she was continually harping on that, even in her head. It didn't mean anything.

"So, you live around here?" Liam asked and then shook his head, laughing. "Of course, you do. You're walking your dog."

The phrase *stranger danger* came to mind, but Arden figured Liam wasn't stalking her. Right?"

When she didn't answer immediately, Liam winced. "Forget I asked. I probably shouldn't be asking a single woman walking alone with her dog where she lives. I actually live two houses down," he said, pointing towards a nice home with a front porch and a lawn that actually looked cared for. A lot of the properties around here had decent lots, but some of it got a little overgrown. A couple of years ago, everybody got a little overambitious when it came to their landscaping, and then they couldn't keep up with it. Liam seemed to have gone minimalistic, and that meant his yard looked nice. Arden's lawn looked pretty much the same because she couldn't really afford to have someone do it for her, and as much as she would love to see her brothers covered in mud as they took care of her place, she couldn't ask that of them. They would do it for her without question, but she liked to have at least some boundaries.

"Oh, I live near here, too. But, um...thanks. For real. For getting Jasper. He saw a rabbit. And, apparently, decided that he didn't want to walk with me anymore. He wanted to run. Without me." She was rambling, and she didn't really know how to stop. But she couldn't help it. She was already out of sorts from having Jasper run off like he had, and with Liam finding him, it was all a little too much for her all at once.

Liam nodded and then looked down at the dog and then back up at her. "So, are we just going to ignore the fact that your white Siberian Husky has a blue face right now? Or is that something special just for Thursdays?"

She wanted to hide under her shirt but knew that would make things even more awkward than they already were. "I was baking, and he kind of found the supplies. One thing led to another, and now we know that Jasper loves food-colored frosting. I'll have to be a little more careful the next time I bake."

Liam laughed, his eyes bright. "You bake? Good to know."

Why would it be good to know? He hadn't called.

She really needed to stop thinking about that. See? It was the last time she was going to do it.

"Well, thanks for saving him. And me. Seriously. I don't know what I would have done if…no, I don't even want to think about that."

"We had a dog when we were younger. He ran out. We caught him in time, but it was a scary few hours. So, I'm glad I was here in the right place at the right time." There was a pause where they were both silent, and Arden didn't know what to say. Thanks? And goodbye? No, walking away right then would mean he would look at her, and she really didn't want him to do that. Or maybe she was worried that he *wouldn't* look at her, and that she was feeling all this awkwardness for nothing.

"Come have coffee with me," Liam said quickly. Her eyes flew open wide.

"Excuse me?"

"Come have coffee with me. There's a café right down the block, one that I try to go to often to work. At least when I don't mind dealing with people. They have an outdoor space, and it's a nice day. I see people bring their dogs all the time."

Arden swallowed hard, reaching down to pet Jasper's

head. "I know the place. I've brought Jasper there before. But we don't need to have coffee, Liam. I get it. Okay?"

See? She could be an adult.

"You get what?" Liam asked, looking genuinely confused.

She needed to find a hole to bury herself in just then. She really wasn't good at this whole thing.

"Nothing. Thank you again."

"I'm not asking you out for coffee just because I helped you find your dog, even though that's part of it. If you don't want to come, I totally get it, but I'd like for you to have coffee with me." He paused. "Please?"

She let out a sigh and studied his face. He was just as handsome as before with the same humor, but there was something different about him today. Maybe something around the eyes that didn't seem so happy, that wasn't as bright as it had been before. Sure, he had been hurting in the hospital, but he was almost care-free then. Now? There was something different about him. Arden wasn't sure why she noticed.

Before she could open her mouth to say, "no," her brain suddenly had a mind of its own. "Okay," she blurted.

"Good." He gestured for her to go ahead of him, and she sighed, grateful that she wasn't wearing her normal bag lady clothes and had actually brushed her hair that morning. At least she looked a little more normal today, except for the fact that she was a little sweaty from running after Jasper. It didn't matter how much she worked out, she always looked a little wrinkled.

They got a table in the corner where Jasper could hang out on the ground out of the way. Liam had gone in to get her a chai latte and an Americano for himself, as well as a bowl of water for Jasper.

She had no idea what was really going on just then. She wasn't good at this whole man/woman thing. But then again, she should probably practice at it, right?

Liam sat down on the other side of the table, and Arden swallowed thickly. He moved really well for a man his size. He had broad shoulders, a thick chest, and a decently slender waist. It looked like he worked out and actually took care of himself. Not that she didn't take care of herself. She just happened to like snuggling on the couch with her dog more than she loved running.

Okay, she preferred just about anything over running.

"Thank you," Arden said quickly, keeping her head out of her thoughts about Liam's body. And the way that his jeans molded to his thick thighs. Or how his ass looked really good when he walked away earlier. *Really* good.

In fact, it reminded her of America's ass—AKA Chris Evans' ass.

She couldn't help it, she was weak.

"You're welcome," Liam said, his voice deep and just a little rumbly.

Damn him.

"So…" she said, letting her voice drift off.

"So," he said softly. Then he cleared his throat. "I'm sorry I didn't call."

She stiffened and did her best to look relaxed even though she knew she looked anything but. Oh, so he was just going to bring it out into the open? That was good. But she had no idea what to say next. "Oh?"

"I had some things happen. Right after I met you. And it kind of messed things up. So, I just wanted to say I'm sorry. I'm not usually such an asshole."

"Oh." Things happened? Well, that wasn't very detailed, but he did apologize. And it wasn't like he had promised that he would call her, or that they had talked more than a few moments while in the hospital. So, she was just going to push it out of her mind. Not everything had to be about her, after all.

"It's okay. Really. Things happen." And they did. Just because she had been feeling down because of her issues didn't mean she had to act weird about it.

"Thanks for being nice about it. I probably would have called myself a few names if it had been the other way around, and you hadn't called me."

"Yeah, I might have called you a few names." She smiled then, and he grinned.

"Touche. So, what do you do?"

"Oh, I do research." That was pretty much the best

way for her to explain what she did because not everybody really understood her job outside of those in the book world. Her brothers barely did.

"Oh? What kind of research?"

Of course, he would ask. Because he was nice. And she hadn't really given him any details. "For authors. I figure out certain details to help them when it comes to their books. That, and I create book compendiums and things. You know, like an outline and a spreadsheet of characters and certain specifics for timelines. It's a lot of paperwork, but I like it."

Liam's eyes widened for a second, but then he just smiled. "That sounds amazing. And very needed."

She nodded, hoping she didn't blush too hard. It was just that voice of his. She felt very awkward. "So, what do you do?"

"I, uh, write things," he said, looking down at his hands and the coffee cup between them. He reached down and scratched Jasper's head, and Arden frowned.

"You write things." She didn't say it as a question, but Liam just shrugged.

"Sorry. Yeah, I'm an author. I'm not usually good at answering that question." He just laughed. "I used to be a model, but I got a little too tired of people calling me 'pretty boy,' and I really didn't like the lifestyle. Plus, it doesn't last when you start showing your age. So, yeah, I'm an author."

"Well, that was a lot just then," she said, but then smiled. "I knew you were pretty. But don't worry. I won't call you pretty boy. But a model? Can I just say wow?"

"It's not as *wow* as you might think. And I was young. But it paid the bills. Now, my other job…"

"Well, I would ask you what your author name is, but you didn't offer it up, so I'm not going to. And I'm not going to ask if I've heard of you or if you're sold in bookstores or whether you write children's books. I won't even say something like, 'I've always wanted to write a children's book.' I've worked with a lot of authors, and I know not to be *that* person."

He looked at Arden then, blinking a few times, and then threw his head back and laughed. She laughed with him and shook her head.

"Yeah, it's amazing how many people get awkward when they realize that you're an author. They ask you things like, 'Oh, like *real* books?'"

"No, the fake ones," Arden said quickly, laughing with him.

"Yeah, then they say things like, 'I have this manuscript I've been working on…' or that they always wanted to be an author and just need to find the time to do it."

"As if it's ever that easy."

"It's not. I love it, but it's not easy at all. I imagine a lot of authors are glad they have you to do some of the work for them." He paused and shook his head. "That's not what I meant."

"Oh, I know. I don't do the work for them, but I *do* help. A cog in the wheel. An integral member of the team. And I'm just fine with that."

Liam laughed. "I bet you your authors are grateful. But since you seem together, my pen name is L.M. Berry. I write historical thriller fiction."

Arden sat back, her mouth going dry as she stared at one of her favorite authors of all time. Yes, her favorite genre was romance, young adult coming in a close second. But L.M. Berry? Seriously, his books made her heart pound. And the hot guy in front of her did the same.

The fact that they were one and the same?

She was pretty sure she was beet red, and she had no idea what the hell to say.

"Arden? Are you okay?"

"Oh my God. No way." She sort of shouted the last part and was thankful that no one was really around to hear her.

"Sorry," she said quickly, holding up her hands. "I swear I'm not going to like, attack you or anything. But I am a fan. Though not a rabid fan." She reached down and ran her hands through Jasper's fur. "Sorry, Jasper. Nothing rabid about you, either."

That made Liam laugh. "So, I take it you've heard of me? That's always weird."

"Oh, I totally get it. I'm sorry. But I love your work. And I'm Literally Addictive Research." She laughed. "I mean, that's my company. I've done some stuff for your books. And I made your book compendium. This is just so weird."

Liam leaned back in his chair, his eyes going bright as he just shook his head. "You helped me. Like seriously helped me with a plot point I was having trouble with like two books ago. I don't remember exactly. I even put you in my acknowledgments. Hell, I didn't know that your company even had a name. Everything was just signed as LAR."

"And I didn't know that L.M. Berry stood for Liam Montgomery Berry."

Liam just shook his head, laughing. "Berry was the name I added at the end for fun after getting drunk and eating berries. Seriously."

Arden's eyes widened and she snorted. "Really?"

"Really. And I think my editor's sending you my next book. This is just insane."

Arden clapped her hands in front of her and did a little chair dance. "Oh, I actually have it now. I'm halfway through, and I'm reading just for pleasure at this point before I go through and pick it apart."

Liam winced. "Ouch."

"Oh, shush. You know by the time I get it I'm just there to help with adding to your notes. You have it down now. But I love it. But what is Nash up to?" she asked before she could help herself.

"You'll just have to wait and see," Liam said.

"So, I guess I can't finagle more answers out of you with coffee?"

"I'm the one who paid, Arden."

"Touche," she said, repeating his word back to him.

They laughed like that for the rest of their time at the café, talking and occasionally stopping to make sure that Jasper was happy. She couldn't help but feel as if today had been one of the best days she'd had in a while.

They finished their drinks, and then he walked her home. She wondered how he could live so close, and she had never seen him in the neighborhood before. But considering that he was an author and probably worked from home just as she did, it made sense. Sometimes, she didn't see people beyond the street she lived on.

"So, this was fun," Liam said, his hands in his pockets again as they stood on her front porch.

"It was a lot of fun," she said to him, smiling.

"Let's do it again," Liam said and then leaned forward and brushed a soft kiss to her cheek.

Not her lips, but very, very close. Close enough that Arden couldn't help but suck in a breath.

She met his gaze, her pulse racing, her mouth parting,

but he didn't kiss her for real, and she was actually grateful. She didn't know if she was ready for that. She didn't know if she was prepared for anything.

But she couldn't help but nod her head and give him a firm, "Yes," even though she didn't know when *again* would be. And even though he hadn't called the first time, she had a feeling he would this time.

And she had his number, too.

Not a bad way to end her day. She went into her house and picked up the book she now knew that Liam Montgomery had written and wondered what would happen next.

CHAPTER 7

*N*ash and Penny were going to give Liam a migraine. No, they had already given him a headache for every single word that had been put on the screen that day.

Writing was hard. He'd always known that. But today? He wanted to reach into his computer and strangle his two main characters.

Maybe it was because he had been lazy up to this point and really only had one main character throughout the series.

Nash had taken center stage for eight books at this point. Each time saving the world and whatever historical artifact he was focused on for the book. Yeah, Liam had put Nash through the wringer, forcing him to lose his brother, his parents, and pretty much any friend he'd ever met and made. Nash had even lost his life once, though he had been brought back via medical intervention. Not by magic, even though Liam had really wanted to make it like that. His publisher hadn't agreed, so CPR and epinephrine had saved him.

Liam had put Nash through almost everything, yet the man was still living and breathing and able to save the world over and over again. Or at least his own part of the world since not every book Liam wrote meant an apocalypse.

Oh, that might be nice…

Liam sat back in his desk chair and rubbed his hand over his face. He needed to shave, the bristles were a little too long. But he was focusing. Or at least *trying* to focus.

What if there was an actual apocalypse that an artifact could prevent? Could he make that work?

Maybe.

He opened up his notes document and added some things for the next book, or perhaps the one that would come out the year after that.

He wrote one book a year and spent almost eight months of it doing research on the historical accuracy for each installment.

Yes, sometimes he got to play with magical realism and time travel in order to make his books work, but even if he did, he really liked to make sure that every piece of historical evidence in the books was real and wouldn't get him into trouble with his readers.

Sometimes, he felt like his fans went back and checked every single little piece of information that Nash gave them. That meant that Liam had to be doubly sure that he didn't fuck it up.

But an apocalypse? An actual one?

Hmm. That could be fun.

He chuckled and closed the window on his second screen, then went back to his original monitor where the cursor blinked, mocking him.

But before he could focus on an apocalypse or whatever was coming next, or even the historical accuracy of what Nash was currently dealing with, he needed to focus on his other main character.

Penny.

She wasn't meant to be a leading character. Nash had had love interests on and off throughout the series. None of them had been too serious, though. The women that Liam added to his books weren't just there so the dudes could look at boobs even in their minds. He hated when authors did that. But Nash had never been in a place to settle down or even think about a serious relationship. Considering that he almost died frequently, those close to him could die, as well. Liam had never wanted to put anyone in that situation. But now, apparently, Penny had other ideas.

Penny was a school teacher, who happened to have an eidetic memory and knew amazing historical facts that Nash needed. He'd started to come to her for more and more help whenever he couldn't figure things out on his own.

Penny was smart, sarcastic, and made Nash figure out exactly what he wanted.

Only Liam couldn't help him figure that out.

The two had been dancing around each other for so long, that Penny now had almost equal page time with Nash. Liam loved it, even if it was hard to get into another character's head the same as he did with Nash. But maybe that was fine. Perhaps he needed to be kept on his toes just like Nash was.

But Liam was coming to the point in the series where he had to make a decision whether Nash was ready to settle down with Penny, or if the two needed to break up —or something worse.

Liam wasn't sure he was ready for something like that, but his publisher was starting to push him in that direction.

They liked the idea of Nash being the bad boy, James Bond type, but that had never sat well in Liam's mind. He had plans for Nash. He imagined that Nash would one day grow up and have a family and, yes, save the world, but he'd be strong enough and in a secure enough place to protect them.

Liam grimaced, saved his document again, and turned off his computer.

A family? What a crock of shit. He couldn't even figure out his own family. How the fuck was he supposed to write Nash a happily ever after?

He was done. Maybe he would just burn everybody in the series to ashes, end it, and write a new one where everybody was depressed and drank too much.

He pinched the bridge of his nose, swallowing a sigh.

"I really need a life," he whispered to himself and then got out of his chair to go and get another glass of water. He would rather have some whiskey in a low-ball glass with a large ice cube, but he wasn't actually going to be day-drinking. Plus, the whole write-drunk-and-edit-sober deal had never been his thing.

He needed a clear mind because, sometimes, his characters mumbled enough.

He didn't need to add drunkenness to that.

Liam poured himself a glass of water and chugged it back while thinking about what he needed to do for the day. Nothing. He literally had to do nothing.

He didn't need to do housework or yard work or plan anything else.

Oh, he probably could, but he didn't want to. He just wanted to sit and wallow in the fact that he had no idea what he was doing.

Timothy Montgomery wasn't his father.

What was he supposed to do with that? How was he supposed to react like everything was fine and that their lying meant nothing?

How was he supposed to deal with the fact that there was some guy named Steve out there who not only hadn't wanted him or his mother but also hadn't cared one way or another that he might one day accidentally bump into his son and not even know it?

Did Liam look like Steve? He'd always thought he looked a little bit like Timothy, but he'd been wrong.

Apparently, his strong jaw, broad shoulders, and quick smile was not from his father. Timothy. Maybe that was Steve?

He didn't know, and since he didn't have the answers, he wasn't really sure what he was supposed to say or do.

As if his mother knew that he was stressing out, his phone buzzed on the kitchen counter. He looked down at it.

He'd put a silly photo of the two of them sticking out their tongues at the camera as her avatar, and he just shook his head when he saw it, wondering what she had been thinking.

Had she been happy? Or had there been some part in the back of her mind that wondered when and if she would tell him that he'd been lied to his entire life.

The whole genetic identity thing? He might have been able to cope with that, especially considering he had cousins who had adopted children or were dealing with second marriages and stuff like that. Yeah, he might have been able to deal with it. Maybe. At least that's what he told himself. But the fact that they had lied to him for over thirty years? His entire life? That, he wasn't sure about. Looking down at the photo, he let it ring one more time before hitting the red button so the call would go to voicemail.

He didn't even feel the little clutch of guilt in his belly.

How was he supposed to feel guilty when he really didn't feel anything at all?

His mom didn't call again, and that made him feel a little something. Was she giving up? Was he making her feel bad? Maybe that's what he needed to do. Because he had been lied to, damn it. Deceived. And everybody expected him to just get over it. Well, fuck that. He wasn't a Montgomery. How was he supposed to get over that?

He looked down at the tattoo on his arm and growled.

He wore the family brand. The crest.

And he wasn't even blood.

Yeah, those brought into the family got it too, those who married in. But Liam hadn't had that choice. He had thought he had been born blood and then found out he wasn't.

Just as he was thinking about what to make for dinner, his doorbell rang, and then it opened as if the doorbell were perfunctory, a warning that they were there.

Of course, they wouldn't care that the door had been locked. They all had fucking keys.

"Go away," he growled from the kitchen, his head in the fridge as he decided what to cook.

"We're not leaving. You're dealing with us," Bristol called out before she walked into the kitchen, her hands full with a covered dish.

Ethan and Aaron followed, both growling at Liam, Ethan's hands filled with beer, Aaron's full of another covered dish, as well as a bowl. He had a bag of chips clutched in the bend of his elbow.

"I see you're just going to have a party here and not ask if that's what I want," Liam said, knowing he was being an asshole. But he deserved to be an asshole. Right?

"Yes, we're bringing you food and beer, and we're going to hang out with you. Oh, poor you, you have people that love you." Bristol set down the dish she held on the counter and then punched him in the arm. "Stop being a jerk. We love you. Let us love you."

"I don't think you need to say it with such conviction," Ethan said dryly as he set the beer down on the counter before slowly taking the bottles out and putting them in the beer fridge below. Liam had added a wine cooler as well as a beer fridge in place of the old trash compactor that he didn't need anymore. It had been a nice addition to his kitchen, but right then, he didn't want it full. He didn't want anyone there either. He just wanted to wallow in his misery. Why didn't the Montgomerys understand that?

That question hit him in the gut, and he swallowed hard.

The Montgomerys. As if he weren't one.

Because he wasn't. Jesus Christ.

"I can act like I'm insane if you want," Bristol said. "But I pretty much am naturally. So, you're going to play video games with us, you're going to eat this seven-layer dip, homemade guacamole, and the buffalo cheese casserole thingy that I made, and you're going to like it. Plus, there's beer. And we know you like beer."

"Buffalo dip casserole thingy?" Liam asked, his lips twitching.

"I forget the name of it. But there's a lot of cream cheese. And hot sauce. And chicken. And it's really good. You're going to have to fight me for it once we're a few beers into our night."

"What if I had plans?" Liam asked, leaning against the counter as he folded his arms over his chest.

Aaron snorted and then looked down at what Liam was wearing. He did the same.

"I don't think slacks with holes in them and a tank top is really showing off your best, Liam. It's not like you were going to leave the house. We know better. You rarely do that, and when you're brooding, it's even worse."

Liam flipped Aaron off and then helped Bristol uncover the dishes.

"I don't want to talk about it," Liam growled.

"We don't have to talk about anything," Ethan said. "We might later. Because once we get a few beers in us, we might want to pry and be all emotional. But we don't have to start out talking about it."

"I feel like he's making fun of women here, but I'm not sure exactly how," Bristol said as she opened up a bag of chips and poured them into one of Liam's large bowls.

"I'm not making fun of women," Ethan drawled. "I'm more making fun of us because that's what we do. We growl at each other and say that we don't want to talk, then we drink, and then that's what we do anyway. We talk."

"I don't want to talk today," Liam assured them. "I had to do enough character building today with Nash. I don't want to deal with it myself."

"So, you don't think you're putting any of yourself into your characters?" Aaron asked, looking completely serious.

"How many *Criminal Minds* episodes do you watch a day?" Liam asked, laughing. Huh, he hadn't known he could laugh today. That was good.

"So, you're saying that you're a serial killer? Or that

you have the chance to become a serial killer? Tell us how that makes you feel," Aaron said, his eyes dancing with laughter.

"He really does watch that show far too much," Bristol put in.

"I can't help it. The first like three seasons were amazing. But then when Mandy Patinkin left, it just went downhill."

"Please do not start talking about Mandy again."

"I can't help it. He was Inigo Montoya. He is one of the greatest actors of all time."

Liam met Ethan's gaze, and the two of them cracked up laughing. Liam's whole body shook as Aaron went on and on about the depths of Mandy Patinkin's characters.

"You seriously need to stop talking about that man," Ethan said, wiping tears from his eyes.

"I can't help it. Plus, I made Liam laugh. I think I win."

Liam narrowed his eyes, not laughing anymore. "Was there a bet to see who could make me laugh? Because I'm going to kick some asses." He narrowed his eyes even further at his sister. "I'll kick your ass, too. Don't think I won't."

Bristol just rolled her eyes and put her hands up in mock surrender. "We didn't actually have a formal bet. We were going to talk about it. But you were laughing, so Aaron wins. And the rest of us do, too. Now, let's bring all this food out to the living room. I do believe Mario Kart is up first."

"Dear God, you're vicious when it comes to Mario Kart," Ethan said, grabbing the guacamole and chips.

"I am. That's why we're going to play it before we get drunk. Because you all curse even worse than you normally do and get violent when you're drunk and playing Mario Kart."

"We can't help it, Mario Kart is a very violent game," Ethan said, and Liam just followed along, shaking his head.

Liam hadn't wanted them there, but he couldn't kick them out of his house.

No, he wasn't over it. Still wasn't sure what to think. But his siblings weren't going to just let him be.

And he would be grateful for that. Later.

Right now? He was going to kick his family's ass at Mario Kart.

About two hours into the game marathon, the curses were flying, the beer was getting low, and all of them were full and at least content.

Liam didn't want to say "happy" because he didn't really feel that way, but they made him laugh over and over again. Plus, watching Ethan get his ass trounced by the rest of them really just made up for everything. Ethan was seriously the worst Mario Kart player.

"Rigged," Ethan shouted. "This whole game is rigged."

Liam just shook his head. "Yes, because Nintendo goes out of their way to make sure that Ethan Montgomery doesn't know how to play. It's all a conspiracy."

"Thank you. Vindication." Liam met Aaron's eyes, and they laughed. Ethan was a computational chemist and had a big, brilliant mind. But the man could not play video games. Watching him play, though? Perfection. It made for a wonderful afternoon.

They paused for a little bit to clean up and start on the next wave of food and games, and Liam looked down at his phone. Since he'd had about three beers, and was feeling a little better, he went to his messages and texted Arden.

Liam: *Are we still on for tomorrow?*

Arden took a little bit to respond, but thankfully, his siblings hadn't returned back to the living room.

Arden: *That's the plan. Having a good night?*

Liam grinned.

Liam: *Yeah, my siblings are over, and we're playing video games like we're twelve.*

Arden: *My siblings are over, and we're playing Scrabble. I would rather play video games, but I lost the coin toss.*

That made Liam laugh, and all three of his siblings gave him weird looks as they walked back into the living room.

Liam: *Not good at Scrabble?*

Arden: *Oh, I'm the best. It helps with my job, after all. But*

I would really rather play something else tonight. I'm glad you're having fun.

Liam: *Well I hope you get to have at least a little more fun soon. Gotta go. Sibs are back, and that means it's time to take them down in the next game.*

Arden: *Kick some butt. See you tomorrow.*

Liam was grinning as he put his phone away and looked up as all three siblings stared at him expectantly.

"What?" Liam asked, looking for his controller.

"Who were you texting?" Bristol asked, sing-songing her voice.

"No one," Liam grumbled. He probably shouldn't have texted Arden when his siblings were around, but three beers made him do silly things.

Or stupid ones.

"It's a girl," Bristol said, checking both of her brothers.

Ethan and Aaron met gazes, and then both grinned back at Liam evilly. The two weren't twins, even though they sometimes acted like it. It was creepy.

"Really? Who were you texting?" Ethan asked and then shrugged. "I bet it's that girl from the hospital."

Liam froze. "Excuse me?"

"Oh, we all saw you with her, even though we were trying to be sly about it. What was her name again?"

Ethan growled and knew it was time to give up. "Her name is Arden. And, yes, it was her. I didn't text her or call her after the hospital for a while for obvious reasons

—that we are not going to get into tonight. Do you get me?" Three nods. "But she lives around the corner, and we met up when I found her dog for her."

"Aw," Bristol said and shut her mouth when Liam narrowed his eyes.

"We're going on a date tomorrow. I just wanted to make sure we were still on. Is that okay with all of you?"

"That's fine with us. We're excited. A date. And Arden is really pretty."

"It's kind of cool that you guys had two little meet-cutes like that," Ethan said and then put his hands in the air when everyone gave him weird looks. "What? I like meet-cutes. Sue me."

"Anyway, I don't think she gets out much, so I wanted to make sure she was still up for going out."

"You don't get out much either, pretty boy," Bristol said, grinning.

"Fuck you," Liam growled and then glared at his brothers. "And fuck both of you, too."

"No thanks," both of the guys said at the same time and then high-fived.

Dear God, they really needed to stop drinking beer, it turned them into imbeciles. All of them. Including himself.

"Anyway, I'm going out with Arden tomorrow, so just let me be, and let's play a game."

"You're not going to tell us anything about her?" Bristol asked, sitting down next to him.

"I don't know a lot yet. I know she has a dog named Jasper, a white Siberian Husky. Although his face was blue at the time because, apparently, he got into her blue food coloring."

Bristol smiled at that. "So, she bakes? Is she a baker?"

"Yes, she bakes, but she's not a baker. She actually works in my industry. We've actually worked together and didn't know it."

"Three meet-cutes," Ethan cheered, and Aaron punched him in the stomach. "Ouch. What was that for?"

"Seemed like the right thing to do at the time," Aaron said casually and then picked up his controller. "Anyway, Arden sounds nice, and it's kind of cool that she works with you."

"Sort of works with me. But it is interesting." Liam paused and wondered why he was going to say the thing he was about to say next. But, why not? Three beers, after all. "I don't think she has a lot of friends, actually. So, even if this doesn't work out, it's kind of nice to know her. You know?"

"Aw," Bristol said again. "You like her."

"I don't even really know her. It's only a date. And I could use just...I don't know. A distraction."

"Don't call her a distraction, bro," Ethan put in. "That's probably the worst thing you could ever do."

"I second that," Aaron added.

"Thirded," Bristol put in. "But I hope you have fun. And I hope she has fun, too. And you guys have fun together and get married and have a bunch of little babies, and everything is wonderful."

"And...that's enough beer for Bristol," Liam said, taking the bottle from her.

"Tequila!" she shouted. The three brothers looked at each other and then broke out laughing, before, of course, breaking out the tequila.

CHAPTER 8

"*P*lease leave. Please, please, please leave."
Arden clasped her hands in front of herself
as she begged her brothers to leave her house. Yes,
begged. Her home. As in they thought they were allowed
to just be there.

Really? Ugh.

"We'll leave. We'll leave." Prior held up his hands, but
Arden noticed that he was not, in fact, leaving. No one
was. All four of her brothers still stood in her living
room, glaring at her.

"You're not leaving," Arden stated.

"Oh, we'll leave."

She waited for Cross to finish his sentence, and she
was not disappointed.

"We'll leave once you tell us exactly what you're doing with Liam Montgomery tonight."

"I don't have to tell you anything," Arden said as she moved forward, trying to push her brothers out of the way. Only they were all more than six feet tall, broad, and very muscly. The exact opposite of her.

Damn them and their good genes. Somehow, she had gotten screwed out of the good ones in the family, and she couldn't just kick them into submission or force them into acting properly. Sadly.

"I shouldn't have even mentioned it. I don't even know why I did."

She would never mention a date again. But they'd caught her unawares, and they'd asked her what she was doing later that night. They'd all come over for lunch because they were big, growing boys that constantly needed food and to be overprotective. They were very lucky she loved them. However, when they asked her what she was doing, she'd muttered something about a date, and it'd been nonstop questions since.

Who was this man? Where did he get the audacity to ask out their baby sister? Didn't matter that Arden wasn't a baby anymore and was perfectly fine going on dates.

They'd wheedled Liam's name out of her because they'd guessed right. Apparently, she didn't meet men enough for them to actually have any question that it was the guy she'd met at the hospital.

Damn them. Damn all of them.

"Just go," Arden said. "There's really no reason for you to be here and freaked out about it. I'm just going on a date. Something I've done before."

"You've gone on a date with Liam Montgomery before?" Macon asked, narrowing his eyes.

"No. This is our first date. So, I should probably shower and actually look decent for him. You know? Not be a total weirdo."

"You're always a weirdo, but you're our weirdo," Nate said, trying to ease the tension. But all Arden wanted to do was kick him. Kick all of them. Kick, kick, kick.

"So, he doesn't think you're good enough if you don't shower and look presentable? What kind of man is this?" Cross asked, growling.

"Oh my God. Just go."

"No, we're not going. I Googled him."

Arden covered her face with her hands. "You did not."

"And if we have our way, we will get that background check done," Prior added. She hoped he was kidding. There had to be laughter in his voice right then, right?

"He used to be a model," Cross added. "A model, Arden."

She lowered her hands and raised her chin. "Are you saying that he's too pretty for me? That he's a model and, therefore, is too good for me? Because I will kick your ass, Cross Brady. I will hurt you, and I will make you rue the day you ever thought I wasn't good enough for Liam freaking Montgomery."

"That is not what I meant," Cross said quickly, putting his hands up.

"Oh, I think you did." She totally didn't think he did, but she was on a roll, and if it got him to leave and apologize for being a butthead, all the better.

"I didn't. I'm just saying, he used to be a model."

"And is there something wrong with models? Are you shaming someone for actually working for a living? Are you shaming him for his past? Because I could start writing a whole list of things all of *you* have done. At least he earned money the old-fashioned way." Arden's eyes widened, and then she burst out laughing.

"Did you just say that we could be hookers?" Prior asked, laughing with her.

"I lost my train of thought. But, anyway, you should go. I need to get ready. I'm not saying that he needs me to be perfect because God knows I'm not."

"You're our perfect baby sister. Don't even think anything else," Macon said quickly.

"And I love you for that. But I'm not perfect. None of us are. There's no such thing as *perfect* other than the word itself. Besides, that's not what I'm talking about. What I'm talking about is the fact that I need to actually shower. And do my hair. And figure out what I'm going to wear. Do all the girly things I like to do, that your dates like to do before you take them out. Because I know you've dated. I have dated people before. I have been on dates. I've had boyfriends." Okay she'd had *one* long-term boyfriend, and it hadn't worked out well, but she wasn't going to add that. Her siblings knew. All too well.

"I've even had sex before," Arden said and watched as all of her brothers paled as one and growled at the same time. "Yes, I've had sex." Oh, this was good. If she kept saying this, maybe they would get grossed out enough to leave. "Lots of dirty, dirty sex. And I may even have sex with Liam Montgomery tonight." Too far. She had gone too far.

"Oh, you won't be having sex with him tonight. Not if we stay here." Nate grinned as he said it, and Arden threw up her hands and sighed. "Stop it. Just go. I know you like to play the overprotective brothers, but you're not actually that annoying. Though if you don't leave now, you're going to cross that line. And I will tell every person I know how annoying you are. I will let any girl you think you might want to date, know that you're so overprotective and rude that you'll just ruin their lives and get all growly and possessive. That you'll become one of those He-Men who beat their chests if their women even dare to look at another man."

"Oh, stop it. We'll go," Cross growled. "And we're not that bad."

"Sometimes, you are. But I love you anyway. Now, go.

Thank you for having lunch with me. And thank you for being amazing and always around. But I need some space. Seriously, I need room to breathe."

"You better need a lot of space. As in space between you and Liam," Prior added. Arden just rolled her eyes.

"That was smooth. Very smooth."

"I try. Now, do we need to go through the rules of you going on dates?" Prior asked.

"No. Because I'm not sixteen. And if you don't get out, I'm going to kick you. I've thought about kicking you all night, and I will make it happen."

"Your little kicks couldn't hurt us," Macon teased. Just because he said that, Arden moved forward and kicked him hard on the shin. Thankfully, she was wearing her house slippers and had just the right amount of edge that tended to bruise if you hit yourself too hard.

"Ow. What the hell, Arden?"

"Oh, did I hurt you?" she asked, not sounding repentant at all. Because she wasn't.

"Okay, now that she's started kicking us, I guess it's time to go." Cross kissed her on the forehead and hugged her before the others did the same. Macon was a little careful around her. Good. She would kick again if she had to.

"I love you. Have a good night."

"Don't have too good of a night," Cross grumbled.

"Oh, stop being a butthead."

"I can't help it. You just bring out the overprotective parts of me."

"I understand that. And it's fine. But if you don't get out, I *will* start kicking. And I will find other things to kick this time. You're very lucky that Jasper is hanging out outside, or he would start barking and force you to go."

Jasper had spent the entire day in the house with Arden and her brothers, and had gone on a walk with them earlier, but he was currently sunbathing in the last rays of light on her back porch, and she wasn't going to bother him. But, if she needed him to get her brothers out of the house, oh, she would totally use him.

"I love you all. Now, go."

With that, she ushered them out the door, making sure to lock it with the deadbolt and the chain after they'd left. They might have keys to her house, but they couldn't get through the little chain without breaking her door. And she knew that none of them actually wanted to deal with the carpentry parts of replacing it, so, that would give her a little bit of time to figure out what to do.

Oh, God. What was she supposed to do? She was going on a date with Liam Montgomery. L.M. freaking Berry. And as much as she wanted to sound all smooth and competent, there was no way she could.

She wasn't good at this whole dating thing. She might have sounded like she knew what she was doing when it came to kicking her brothers out of the house and thinking that she knew the plan for the night, but really, she knew nothing. And she was seriously stressing out.

And because she was stressing out, she needed someone to talk her down.

She quickly went to her computer and opened the messaging service for a social media site.

She didn't have any friends in real life. At least, not in person. That was because once you got sick over and over again, people sort of pulled away. They didn't do it on purpose. They weren't mean about it. But life happened. The more times you had to say no to invites, the more those invites stopped coming. It was just life.

And because Arden couldn't be relied on to be there for someone, they weren't always there for her.

She didn't hold that against them, and she didn't really have any regrets. It was hard to do when she couldn't really control what her body did.

But she had a few online friends. They were the ones from her book world, and each of them had their own chronic illnesses. One had rheumatoid arthritis, one had fibromyalgia, one had multiple sclerosis, and the other had what her doctors thought might be Lyme disease or something similar. All of them had been through years of diagnoses and failures, the same with Arden.

The fact that they had formed their own little group

of online friends who tended not to leave the house just meant that they had connections.

Connections they might not have found without the internet.

Her online friends were her real friends. She just didn't see them.

She quickly sent out an SOS, and Lacey, her friend with multiple sclerosis—though she was far more than her label—was the only one on.

Lacey: *What's up?*

Arden: *I have to get ready for my date tonight, and I have no idea what to wear.*

Lacey: *Well, what are you doing? And oh my God, a date. I can't wait for info. If you can get a photo without acting like a creeper, I would totally appreciate it.*

Arden grinned.

Arden: *I think we're going out for Italian. Just a cute little restaurant nearby. So nothing too fancy. But probably not jeans and a T-shirt.*

Lacey: *Dark jeans could work. Or your leggings with a cute tunic. There was that one photo that you posted of you in that flowery tunic that matched your black flats you just bought. That might work.*

Arden grinned. See? She had friends. Even ones that lived across the country in different time zones.

Arden: *Okay, I'll figure it out. I hope.*

Lacey: *And pics?*

Arden: *That might be weird on the first date. But maybe for a message. Just not publicly.*

Lacey: *Oh, I know the rules. Never publicly. Never weird. Have fun tonight. And have a blast. And keep all your spoons!*

"Okay, time to get ready to go," she spoke to herself as Jasper came in, prancing just a bit. He had already gone on two walks that day and had spent some time wrestling with her brothers on the ground so, hopefully, he should be okay at home alone for a couple of hours. She really hated leaving him, but he would be fine. As long as she wasn't gone for too long. And it wasn't like she was going to be gone all night. That was so not what her plans were for the night. She might have joked with her brothers about it, but there was no way.

She was just about to head to her bedroom when someone rang the doorbell.

"I swear to God if it's one of my brothers..." she muttered to herself before looking through the peephole and frowning.

She opened the door as far as the chain would allow, grateful that she'd also locked the glass screen, and frowned. "Hi, can I help you?" The woman looked familiar, but Arden couldn't remember where she might've seen her.

"Hi, I'm Bristol. Bristol Montgomery. Liam's sister. I sort of saw you at the hospital that one day. And I know this is super weird, and I'm going to explain everything. I promise."

Arden just blinked. "Okay, Liam's sister? How…how did you know where I live?" She slowed down the words, ready to close the door and run if she needed to. Jasper was at her side, his ears pricked as he let out a little warning growl.

Bristol's eyes widened, and she took a step back, her free hand moving up into the air in surrender. Her other hand was full of a bag, and Arden was a little worried. This was strange.

"Okay, this is weird. So, my brother's super-organized, and he put your address in his phone. Apparently, he figured out where you live because he saw you after a little jog with your dog, Jasper, or something? Anyway, I stole the phone to figure out where you lived so I could stop by and see you and ask if you needed help getting ready for your date tonight because Liam kind of mentioned that he didn't think you had a lot of friends. I know, that sounds horrible. I didn't mean it like that, and I'm so sorry. Can you get your dog to stop growling at me so I can explain everything better?" Bristol basically said that all in one breath, and so quickly that Arden had trouble keeping up.

"He said I didn't have any friends?" Arden asked, incredulous.

"No. He said he didn't think you got out much. But he

didn't actually mean it like that, because now it sounds like he's a jerk. He doesn't get out much either. He only meant that we should stop haranguing him for details about you. I took it upon myself to see if you needed help getting ready. And I'm nosy and just wanted to make sure you knew that everything is good for tonight. And now that I'm standing here looking at your dog that could probably bite my face off, and your expression as you look at me like I'm an insane person, I realize I *am* that person. I'm just gonna go. We'll never tell Liam what I just did, right?"

Arden let out a laugh, completely stunned and a little confused.

"Let me get this straight. You were afraid I didn't have any friends because of something Liam said, so you wanted to help me get ready for a date with your brother?"

"Yes. And this is insane. I should just go."

Well, Arden had heard worse. She was probably making a mistake, but from the sheer look of horror on Bristol's face when she realized what she'd actually done, Arden couldn't help but laugh, release the chain, and unlock the screen door. She patted Jasper's head, and he moved back, giving her and Bristol some space.

"Okay, let's start over. Because I remember you from the hospital, even if I only saw you in passing. Liam's only said good things about you, so let's pretend that this is normal," Arden said. Because, frankly, Bristol looked mortified, and like she could use some friends herself. Plus, helping Arden figure out what to wear beyond what Lacey had said would be helpful. Or maybe she was also losing her mind much like Bristol had just claimed to be doing.

"Oh, thank God. Just don't tell Liam I did this."

Arden laughed, shaking her head. "Oh, I'm pretty sure this is going to be the main topic of conversation for tonight," Arden said, laughing. "Hi. I'm Arden Brady." She gestured to her dog. "And this is Jasper." Jasper let out a bark, sniffed at Bristol's hand, and then pranced away back to the back yard where he would most likely finish sunning himself for the evening.

"Well, Jasper doesn't think you're a threat. So, welcome to my home."

"Oh, thank God. I'm such an idiot. I'm Bristol Mont-gomery. Like I said before. And Liam didn't say anything bad about you. I promise. We were all at his house last night playing video games."

"I know, he told me."

Bristol grinned. "And he told us that he told you. He was texting when we walked in, and we totally grilled him for all the details that we could. And because of that, he mentioned that you worked from home and in the same field as him, and that you guys lived close to one another."

"I do. All of the above."

"Anyway, he mentioned that you worked the same way as he does, which in my mind meant you rarely leave the house and probably don't actually get to talk with a lot of people in person. I am probably completely wrong. And if you'd like to push me out of the house now, that is totally fine. I'm really just being nosy."

"This is the weirdest thing ever, but I guess that's cool."

"Well, I did steal your address from him, he didn't give it to me. So, technically, I'm a horrible person right now, but I wanted to see if you wanted to do girl things to get ready for the night. And see if you needed to talk about anything. Plus, I'm super pushy, it's kind of a Montgomery thing."

"He mentioned there are like forty of you, right? That's a lot of push," Arden said, a little shaky.

Bristol laughed. "Oh, I think there's more of us than that by now. Though I am one of the pushier ones. But my cousin Maya, down in Denver? She would probably be your best friend already, and you guys would be doing each other's nails by now. I did bring nail polish, but your nails already look done, so I guess I don't need that."

Arden just laughed, wondering if she should just live in the moment. She didn't do that often, and Bristol didn't seem like a psychopath. Though that was probably what all victims thought before the serial killer got them.

"Okay, I guess."

"Liam really didn't mention that you needed friends. But…" Bristol trailed off, and Arden shook her head.

"I believe you. But maybe something in the way he said it made you think that. He's not wrong. I am sort of a recluse and like to stay in my house."

"He's the same way. Plus,"—Bristol sighed—"he's in a weird place. I can't talk about it because that's for him to talk to you about, but I wanted to make sure you didn't need anything and, well, you know I'm weird."

Arden laughed. "I'm pretty weird, too."

"Good. Then we can be best friends. As long as you like…don't actually hate my brother by the end of this. But we're not going to talk about that. We're just going to be friends. Anyway, I brought bourbon creme hot off the black market. Okay, not really, but it used to only be available in Kentucky. But I have my ways."

Bristol pulled out a black bottle with brown and caramel coloring on it, and Arden wondered what the hell she had gotten into. Was it too late to call the police?

"Um, I don't really drink a lot," Arden put in. She didn't mention that it was because it sometimes messed with her meds because, as much as she was trying to go with the flow with this whole Bristol thing, it was still a little weird, and she didn't want to show the woman all of her insecurities and weaknesses on their first meeting.

"Oh, it's fine. I figured you could just keep the bottle

in your house if you like it. If not, I can take it back with me. But if you want help getting ready, I'm here."

"Well, I guess you can help me pick out what to wear. Because I have no idea what I'm doing."

"Well, I'm here to help. My ex-girlfriend is a beauty blogger and influencer, and she helps me figure out what I'm supposed to wear, too."

"Your ex helps you?"

"Yeah, we just weren't a good fit as a couple, but she loves dressing me, so it's what I do. And I can probably help you out, if you want. But I can also leave if it gets to be too much. Because I am a bit much sometimes. Believe me, all of my brothers and my best friend, Marcus, tell me that all the time."

Arden just laughed and let the other woman have her way.

It was weird. Very weird. In any other circumstance, this would have felt a little like stalking, and a bit like Arden had hit her head. But there was just something about Bristol that made it seem...okay. Probably any other person on the Earth would have made this completely strange and nonsensical, but Bristol was just amazing. She put Arden at ease and made her laugh.

In the hour that Bristol was there, Arden was fluffed and cleaned and buffed and made adorable. She'd even been put in something from the back of her closet, similar to what Lacey had picked out, just with a little more pizzazz.

And she borrowed Bristol's earrings, which could be odd, but this evening had already been bizarre enough, so it wasn't *too* bad.

In the end, Arden felt like she had made a friend.

There was just something about Bristol Montgomery.

It was probably the Montgomerys in general. After all, she was going on a date with one of them in the next twenty minutes.

"Okay, you have my number, and I even put my address in your phone just in case you want to show up at my house randomly to get payback or something."

"No, if payback is needed, I'd probably send one of my brothers," Arden said with a laugh.

Bristol's eyes brightened. "You have four brothers, right?"

"Yes, but I wouldn't wish them on my worst enemy."

"They can't be that bad. I know brothers."

"They aren't bad. Actually, they're pretty amazing and sweet and caring. They're just overprotective, and I'm in a tiff with them right now, so I don't want to inflict them on you."

"I think you mean inflict me on them, but that's fine."

"Thank you for this."

"Thank you for letting me in the door. As soon as I got here, I realized that what sounded like a good plan in my head was probably actually the worst plan in the history of plans. Thank you for not calling the police on me. Or Liam. Even though I know you're going to talk about it with him later. I'll deal with the consequences of that then. But you look amazing, and I hope you have a wonderful time. Anything that makes Liam smile right now is worth the scolding I'll likely get later."

"Thanks again," Arden said, ignoring what Bristol had mentioned in passing. It seemed that Liam Montgomery truly had some secrets, but Arden wasn't surprised by that. After all, he'd mentioned that he had some stuff to deal with. And it seemed Bristol knew what it was.

Arden said goodbye to the other woman, made sure Jasper was fed, and then looked down at herself, wondering if she was making a mistake.

Today had already been weird, and she was afraid what might happen once Liam showed up. Would things get stranger?

The doorbell rang again, and Arden went to open it, her breath catching when she looked at the very sexy, very real Liam Montgomery on the other side of the door.

CHAPTER 9

*L*iam leaned back in his chair and couldn't keep his eyes off the woman on the other side of the table.

He had known that Arden was beautiful, pretty, gorgeous. He had known she was stunning.

It didn't matter that the first time he had seen her, she'd had a rash on her face and on her arms, and had been sick enough to warrant a visit to the hospital. It hadn't negated the fact that he found her beautiful.

In fact, it was her inner strength and the beauty that came from that smile of hers even when he knew she was in pain that had turned him towards her in the beginning.

And then, seeing her run after her dog, panting and

laughing and trying to look stern...that had just sent him over the edge.

Yes, she was beautiful, but her personality made her even ten steps hotter.

At least, that's what he thought.

Because as soon as she had opened her door earlier that night when he showed up at her house? Yeah, he had just about fallen to his knees in thanks.

She wore tight black pants that didn't really look like jeans, but he knew they were because of the seams. Over that, she had on this blousey thing that tucked in right at her hips and made her boobs look perfect. Not that he was staring at her chest. He did an excellent job of not doing that because he wasn't a lecher. At least, mostly.

Her cute feet were tucked into these little flats that just made her look adorable and yet sexy at the same time.

He had thought a little black dress, fuck-me heels, and sexed-up hair was possibly the hottest thing in the world. But he was wrong. Arden in cute black jeans, a soft top, and adorable shoes was apparently what turned him on.

Either he had reached an age where this was his new way to judge hotness, or, Arden was special.

As she smiled at something he said, he had a feeling it was a mixture of both.

It was all Arden.

Because she was just so damn strong. No matter what she did, she was strong.

He knew that she still had to be hurting, still had bad days—even though he didn't know exactly what those days entailed or what made her hurt. But she was there with him, even when his head wasn't totally in the game because of everything going on in his life.

He reminded himself that this was only their first date. And Arden was simply a distraction. That's what he needed. A step away from his worries, his thoughts, and frankly, his family.

Arden was perfect for that. Maybe he could be a distraction for her, too, because he had a feeling she needed one.

"So, shall I do the whole tell-me-about-yourself thing?" Liam asked, smiling. He shook his head and continued. "I'm really not as smooth as my brothers would have you believe if you met them. Okay, they would probably actually call me *pretty boy* and other things, but I'm not going there."

Arden laughed, leaning forward over her plate. "My brothers pretty much think the same of me. Though they don't call me *pretty boy.*"

"Yeah, I probably shouldn't have mentioned that. Ever. If we could just not use that name again, that would be great."

"I don't know. I think if I shouted 'pretty boy' across

the grocery store if I ever saw you there, it could be a thing. You could just endorse your checks like that and sign off your emails that way. We'd all know who we were talking to."

"I hate them. Seriously."

"You're the one who brought it up."

"Just saying."

"Well, how about you tell me something about yourself?"

"Like what?"

"I don't know. How did you get into your work?" He winced. "You don't have to answer that. I hate answering how I knew I wanted to be a writer."

"Oh, how did you know you wanted to be a writer?" Arden asked, her eyes twinkling.

"See, I keep opening myself up to these things."

"You really do. But I'll answer the question if you do."

"Deal."

They stared at each other, then laughed.

"I guess I should go first?" Liam asked, shaking his head.

"Why not."

"I loved reading as a kid, and then I found myself hating it when I was in school because they kept making me read these books that weren't really my cup of tea."

"Oh, I hated the required reading in school. I swear I never understood exactly what the teacher wanted me to learn. All that symbolism that really wasn't. Was the author saying that the curtains were blue?"

Liam continued. "Yeah, whenever I find myself describing the room that the character goes into and I'm actually worried about the color of the wallpaper, I know that I really need to push it out of my head and just get to the character's motivation."

"Thank God."

"Anyway, I kind of quit reading for fun because I was forced into it. And while I was a teen, I was actually working on some modeling gigs. Not a lot, but enough. And then I was working full-time right out of high school. I took a couple of years off from school and didn't go directly to college because I was making good money. And I liked it. Much to my parents' dismay."

He held back a wince at that, not one to get into the whole who his parents were and what they meant to him thing. Because, frankly, he couldn't even formulate words about what he was feeling, and this was just a first date. Only a distraction. He had to keep telling himself that. He didn't need anything serious, not right then. Maybe not ever with the way that his mind was going.

"I really need to Google your old modeling days." She smiled as she said it. "As it is, you don't have an author photo, which I think is very weird in this day and age."

Liam just shrugged. "It started off because I didn't want people to remember me from my modeling days.

Not that they would, but we know how Google is. And I don't really go to a lot of signings, even though I should. Though with my next book, keeping those two worlds separate will be a moot point."

"Really?"

"Yeah, I'm finally being forced to go on tour, something I'm a little worried about. But the last book hit the *New York Times* somehow. So, here we are."

"I remember when you hit. It was a big deal."

"Yeah, kind of a really big deal. It makes me happy, and a little scared at the same time. You know? The next step and all that? Anyway, my photo's going to be slapped up on my website and on my social media that the publisher runs for me. So, that means people will figure out who I am and who I used to be if they want to Google things like that."

"And we like to Google things like that," Arden agreed.

"Great. But how did I start? Well, I got bored on set sometimes, and it wasn't like I was old enough to really do anything. At least legally."

"I won't ask. Don't worry. Yet."

"Thank you for that reprieve. Anyway, I picked up a book that was sort of suspense, and sort of historical fiction all at the same time. I fell in love with it and needed to read the whole series, even though I started at book fourteen like an idiot."

"I hate when I accidentally start a series in the wrong place."

"It's the worst. However, I did find the rest of the series and then found a bunch of other authors. And I just kept reading and reading. And then I went to college once I decided I didn't want to model anymore. While I was there, even with the required reading, I just *kept* reading."

"What's your degree in?"

"Business Management and Business. Kind of general because I didn't really know what I wanted to do. I took this creative writing class that I fell in love with, and I just kept going. One thing led to another, and in a drunken stupor, I decided that I was going to find an agent and see if it actually worked."

"A drunken stupor?" she asked, her brow raised.

"Yeah, not really, but that's how it felt. I was rejected I think eighteen times, but the nineteenth, they wanted to see a partial manuscript. And that's who I stayed with. I'm very lucky, I know that. But…I like what I do."

"You're lucky that you like what you do, but it's not just luck that got you here. I've read your work, sometimes even before it's published. You have talent, and you work hard. It's not just luck."

"Thanks for that. Now, your turn to answer."

"Mine's pretty simple. Or, really not. I got a Liberal Arts degree. Yes, I know, so helpful. But I also did a dual major with English. I wanted to be a teacher, and I wanted to work with kids and maybe even high school students, depending on where I was when I finished school. And I wanted to do what I loved. Deal with books. Because, like you, I hated reading what was required of me in school, but I still actually read on the side. I thought that maybe if I was that English teacher, I could help myself and other students love what the state required us to read. But it didn't work out like that."

Liam frowned. "Why?"

Arden played with the pasta on her plate, rolling a meatball around the edges.

"I got sick. And that meant I couldn't finish school when I wanted to. When I finally did, I didn't have the energy to get my teaching certificate. I couldn't get out of bed some days, and I couldn't really be consistent. Nobody could rely on me. And it sucked."

Liam leaned forward and gripped her hand, giving it a squeeze. "I'm sorry. I won't ask what happened, but I will ask…is it still going on?"

She met his gaze and gave him a sad smile.

"It'll always be going on. I have lupus."

Liam blinked. "That's an auto-immune disease, right?"

"Yes, lupus is where my immune system pretty much becomes hyperactive and attacks my healthy tissue. It attacks everything it can. Kidneys, my blood, my skin, my joints, my heart, even my lungs. All of that is fair game. I have to deal with pancreas issues and liver issues. Lots of stomach issues. Some days, I just don't have the energy to get out of bed. Some days, I feel like I'm doing great and, suddenly, I'll crash in the middle of the day and not be able to do anything. Most of the time, I can focus and get things done as long as I don't move around too much if I'm in the middle of a flare or move around too little if I'm not, but my eyes can give out, and everything hurts. All the time. So, yeah, lupus sucks. I had it when I was younger, and I'm going to have it for the rest of my life. And because of the nature of the disease, it comes with a whole host of other ailments and what they call sister-diseases. There are blood tests for lupus itself, but because of the medications they give you for the hundred different symptoms, it's hard to diagnose because it causes false negatives. It just sucks."

Liam swallowed, trying to comprehend everything that she had been through even at her young age. What did one say to that? Did you tell the person they were strong? Because that just felt like a cop-out. Of course, Arden knew she was strong. She fought every day.

So, he said the only thing that he could, something that was true.

"I'm sorry. That sucks."

She snorted and smiled brightly, the expression actually reaching her eyes. "Yeah, that's a good word for it. I hate it, but it's my life now. The first time you met me? It was because the sun gave me a flare and I had a reaction to it. The *sun*. I was out with my brothers at an outdoor concert, and even though I was slathered in sunscreen and wore a hat, I still had a reaction. So, I needed to get an infusion to hydrate and calm my immune response. Everything hurt, and I had cramps all over my body. My joints felt like they were trying to fall off. But, that's just life. And it sucks, like you said. But it's life." She shrugged, and he scooted his chair over just a bit more so he could wrap his arm around her shoulders.

"Well, you're still here."

"True."

"I have no idea what to say. I really suck at this. For a man who uses his words for a living, I don't know what to say."

"There's nothing *to* say. You're not supposed to deal with anything like this, especially at my age. Or any age. But I do. And, because I do, and it took forever for us to actually diagnose it and determine that I couldn't do what I wanted to do, I sort of fell into this job. At first, I was taking editing courses to get certified. I thought maybe I could become a freelancer and work that way. I still have the certification, but I got so busy with the other parts of my job that I haven't actually done a lot of editing over the last couple of years. I met a publisher online, and we hit it off, and things just worked out for me. I created a whole business where I can work from my bed if I need to. Which is good. Because, sometimes, I just can't get out of bed." She sighed and played with her meatball again. "Probably not the best thing to tell you on a date. I mean, me talking about the fact that my body is trying to attack itself and sometimes I'm just too tired to get out of bed. Oh, so sexy, right?"

She rolled her eyes, but Liam reached out and cupped her face. "I think you're pretty damn sexy. I thought it earlier, about how I even found you attractive when you were in your hospital bed. And you're even hotter now because I know who you are. At least, parts of you. I'm sorry you have to go through this, but I still see you as a woman, if that helps."

He winced. "I really suck at words."

Arden just smiled and leaned forward so her forehead rested against his. "You don't. The fact that you just said you see me as a woman? Even when sometimes I feel like I'm just a decaying corpse? Yeah, I think I like that."

"Decaying corpse?" Liam asked, laughing.

"What? Sometimes, I just have a bad day. Now, do you want this meatball? I could roll it towards you like *Lady and the Tramp* if you want."

That made Liam laugh. He shook his head. "You know, I was having *Lady and the Tramp* vibes the whole time we were eating that pasta."

"Yeah, but I still think I'm going to do the whole meatball thing. I'll save it for Jasper, though. He was a good dog today."

"Sounds like a plan."

And then Liam leaned forward and barely brushed his lips over hers, just a soft caress. Because he could.

She sucked in a breath, and he looked at her, keeping his eyes open as he pulled away.

"What was that for?" she asked, her voice breathy.

"Because I wanted to. Because...why not?"

"Why not?" she repeated, her voice a whisper.

It didn't matter what was going on with him or even her. Sometimes, a person just needed a moment like this. A single second where they could be themselves— not their pasts or whatever might have brought them down.

And Liam didn't mind that. Not in the least.

When they got back to Arden's place, Liam wasn't sure what would happen next. Then again, when it came to Arden and everything that had happened over the past few weeks with him, he never knew what was going to happen next.

"Tonight was nice," Arden said as Liam turned off the engine and they got out of his car.

Nice. Well, good to know he still had it.

"Nice?" He growled, not realizing he was actually doing it until the sound came out.

Her eyes widened, and she lowered her head, smiling.

"Nice is good. Nice is really good. I haven't had nice in a while."

He was in front of her in two steps, his hand on her face, lifting her chin up so they could meet eyes.

"I haven't had nice in a while, either."

And then he lowered his head, brushing his lips across hers, just a little bit, not wanting to leave.

When she parted her lips for him, he groaned and delved into her mouth a bit more, deepening the kiss ever so slightly before he had to pull away, remembering exactly where they were. They were not inside her house. No, they were in *front* of her house, in her driveway, where any neighbor could look out at any moment. And considering the neighborhood they lived in, someone was probably watching.

"I guess I should stop kissing you where anybody can see," Liam whispered, his mouth a breath from hers.

She pulled back from him, and he hid his disappointment, even as she looked at him, her eyes dark with pleasure, her mouth swollen from his kisses. "Maybe you should come in," she whispered.

Liam froze and swallowed hard. "Are you sure?"

"We already talked about life being short. So, why don't you come in?"

And then Liam was kissing her again, knowing his answer was in the kiss, and in his touch.

He couldn't wait to see what happened next.

CHAPTER 10

*A*rden had told herself she wouldn't sleep with Liam on their first date. She had clearly been wrong. But, if she thought of their coffee together that one afternoon as a date, and their meeting in the hospital as the first date, this could be their *third* date.

It totally counted.

She pulled away from him, catching her breath before wordlessly going to unlock her door. Liam pressed in, his body a warm, oh-so-hot wall behind her. As she opened the door, Jasper trotted by, and she remembered that she couldn't just sleep with Liam right then. She had responsibilities, ones that meant she might ruin the mood.

"Um…" she whispered as Jasper glared at Liam. Well, this was going to be interesting. "I need to let him out. And, uh, put his meatball in the fridge. Sorry."

Liam just chuckled, wrapped his hand around the back of her neck—dear God that was hot—and kissed her hard on the mouth. "I'll let him out, you go take care of the doggie bag." He laughed again. "Ha, that's the first time it makes sense."

"I know, right? I'll be quick."

"Same. Then? Then we might not be so quick."

She heated from the inside out as she left, Jasper trotting along behind Liam even as he gave her a look over her shoulder. Jasper, not Liam. Liam apparently knew what he wanted, and Arden's overprotective dog had apparently taken cues from her brothers.

No, she wouldn't be thinking about them tonight. Not even a little. She quickly put away the bag, then ran to her bedroom to make sure everything looked okay. She wasn't messy, but she hadn't really been expecting to have a man over. Before she could clean up her spare blanket and hide the other bra that she'd tossed away when Bristol had told her to change, a strong arm wrapped around her waist even as the sound of the door snicking closed hit her ears.

"Hi," she whispered breathily.

"Hi." Liam kissed her neck, and her knees went weak, her body warming even as she ached between her legs.

"Where were we?" Liam asked, his voice a growl.

Arden arched into him, her whole body shaking. There was just something about him. Even when she felt like she was at her lowest, Arden couldn't help but want him, she couldn't help but need him.

He just made her feel.

Yes, that was it. Liam made her feel.

"I think we were right here," Arden whispered against his mouth. Then he was kissing her again, his hands moving along her back, slowly lowering to cup her ass.

She let out a breathy moan, arching into him as the hard line of his erection pressed into her belly.

Just thinking about how long and thick he was against her made her suck in a breath.

Because, dear Lord, if what she felt under the lines of his jeans was him, she was in trouble. The best kind of trouble. The sort that she couldn't wait to get into.

His tongue teased her, and she opened more, loving the taste of him, and the way he explored her mouth—gentle at first, then with a little nibbling and then some touching.

She heated from the inside out, her nipples pebbling, and her core aching. She wanted him inside her, and she wasn't even sure how she had gotten to this point. One moment, they were talking about meatballs. The next, she couldn't breathe without wanting him.

This was everything, and yet not enough.

She rubbed her thighs together, moaning again.

Liam let out a rough chuckle and slid his denim-clad

thigh between her legs, forcing her to arch for him even more.

He kept kissing her, one hand on the back of her head, forcing her mouth exactly where he wanted it, the other firmly planted on her butt, pushing her closer as she slowly rocked against his thigh. The seam of her jeans rubbed on her clit, and it almost made her cry out.

She closed her eyes, trying to keep her breathing steady as he slowly rocked. He moved with her, one wave, one roll, and then another.

She couldn't breathe, couldn't focus, and then his hand was suddenly between her cheeks on her butt, slowly running down the seam of her jeans to meet his thigh and then back up again. Stroke, stroke, stroke, even as he rocked into her. And then she came, just like that, a hair-trigger. She couldn't say anything, just rolled her head back as she shook on his thigh.

When she could open her eyes again, she saw that he was grinning, his eyes dark with lust. She knew she was blushing.

She had just come by dry-humping his thigh, and she had no idea what to say about that.

"You're so beautiful when you come," he growled.

Arden swallowed hard. "Well, that was a little quicker than I thought. Sorry."

"Nothing to be sorry about. But I think that means I'm going to start counting. One." He kissed her hard, and she rocked into him again. "Now, let's see how we can get to two."

Counting? Oh, she was not going to last the night, not with the wicked gleam and the determination in his gaze.

"Are we going to count with you?"

"We can, but first, it's all about you. And a second. And maybe a third."

She swallowed hard, and then he was kissing her again, this time slowly moving her back to the edge of the bed.

His fingers went to the bottom of her tunic, slowly raising it up and over her head. She swallowed hard, wondering how this was happening. How was she standing in front of him in just her bra and her jeans, her shoes toed off when she walked into the bedroom?

"Stop thinking so hard. It's just you and me. Just right now. Anytime you need a break, I'm here. If you need me to stop, you tell me. But for now? It's just you and me." He growled the words, so low and deep that it went straight through her, making her shiver, her breasts heavy and pushing against her bra. And then his hands were behind her back, and her bra was on the floor, his mouth on her nipples.

She slid her hands through his hair, arching into him as he lapped at her nipple, using his hand to play with her other breast.

He paid such gentle attention—nibbling, sucking,

using his tongue in a way that she hadn't thought possible. And then his mouth moved over to her other breast, and he paid equal attention to that side, sucking and molding.

She was a bundle of nerves, her whole body shaking as he pressed her breasts together and licked between her nipples, his eyes filled with dark need and laughter as their gazes met.

"I love your tits," he growled. "So, fucking fuckable."

"Fucking fuckable?" she asked, snorting.

"It's a thing. And maybe I'll fuck them later. But first, I need you."

She really didn't have anything to say to that because he was suddenly on his knees, kissing down her stomach and over the seam of her jeans, biting at her belly button. Her hands slid over his shoulders again, and then he was undoing her pants, forcefully pulling them down to get them over her butt, taking her panties with them.

Then she was naked in front of him, self-conscious and blushing all over.

But she didn't have enough time or mental energy to feel embarrassed about it. In the next breath, Liam's mouth was on her, slowly spreading her with his fingers as he licked at her clit and lapped at her.

She shuddered, reaching behind her so she could grip the bed to steady herself. Her knees were actually weakening as he slowly licked, licked, and licked some more.

He teased her, blowing cool air over her, and then changing hands to warm her as he played with her clit and lapped at her quickly.

She came again in a blast of heat and stars and tried to focus. Attempted to reach out to him, call his name. But there was nothing.

There was just him, just them.

And then she was on her back on the bed, and Liam's shirt was off.

She sucked in a breath, her focus fully on him now.

He was a thing of beauty. Arden had known Liam was hard and built, but she hadn't known he was like *that*. She didn't actually know people in real life who had eight-packs. Not just a six-pack, but an eight. The ridges of his abdomen were so defined that every time he breathed, sucked in an inhale, she could see them working. He had that V, the Adonis lines that went beneath his jeans, and she couldn't wait to see exactly what they pointed to.

His shoulders were broad, his muscles perfectly sculpted, and she just licked her lips, wanting to touch every inch of him.

"You keep looking at me like that, I'm going to come in my jeans like a teenager."

She looked down at his groin and licked her lips. "So, you better take them off," she said with a laugh. Liam grinned.

"Okay, you really need to stop talking like that." But then he undid his belt and shucked his jeans.

His cock sprang free, slapping his belly and leaving behind a little trail of fluid on his skin.

He was long, thick, and hard.

And he was about to fill her.

A lot.

Dear God.

"Wow," she whispered. "I mean, it was wow before, but are you sure that's going to fit?"

"Seriously? You say the sweetest things. Now, how do you want me?"

Before she could answer, his head was between her legs once more, one of her thighs over his shoulder as he sucked her to orgasm again.

Dear God, the man could do things with his tongue. She knew he had a way with words, knew he could use his mouth to say wonderful things, but his mouth on her core just then?

Dear. God.

Before she could even come down from her orgasm, Liam was bent over the bed, rustling for something in his pocket, and then there was a condom on his cock, and his hands were on her hips.

"Got to be safe. Only got one, though. I better make it last."

"Okay, but I definitely think I can go again." She knew

her words were breathy, so she gripped her breasts, pinching her nipples to keep herself in the moment and force herself to focus.

"Okay, you *really* need to stop doing that," Liam said, gripping the base of his cock. "That…that's going to make me come."

She grinned and rolled her nipples between her fingers. Liam groaned, slowly cupping his balls since the rest of him was covered.

But before she could make him come in his condom just by standing in front of her, he rolled them so he was on his back, and she was over him.

"I want to see you play with those tits as you slide over me. Come on, baby, come and ride me."

She licked her lips again, and he groaned. Then she let go of one of her breasts so she could slowly guide him into her.

It had been a long time, and though she used toys, this was probably going to hurt.

Liam must have realized that she was going slow for a reason, so he reached around. He kept one hand on her hip to steady her, but his other hand was on her clit, his thumb rolling slightly until she got impossibly wetter.

She met his gaze, forcing herself not to let her head fall back, and then she was fully seated on him, his entire length inside her, filling her, stretching her.

"I can't. I need to move." She gasped.

"Then, move. Ride me," Liam instructed.

And so she did. She rocked, slowly at first, and then quicker. She lifted herself up and over him, using one hand to brace herself on his chest as she played with her breast with the other.

Liam kept his thumb on her clit and made her come for the fourth time. And then a fifth.

She couldn't even remember counting, couldn't remember much of anything, and then she was on her back, and he was pounding into her, the muscles in his neck and shoulders straining as he leaned forward and took her lips. And then he came, both of them sucking in breaths as she tried to figure out precisely what was happening and where they were.

But it was no use.

This was Liam. And this was them. And Arden couldn't focus. Couldn't do anything.

Because that had been the best sex she'd ever had.

Though she knew it was more than sex. More than just hot heat. With what they had shared during dinner and how things had just gone, it was obvious.

But while he might be fun for the moment, she would do her best to shield her heart. This had to be just sex. It had to be.

CHAPTER 11

*L*iam looked down at the hose in Arden's hand and raised a brow. "You want me to what?"

"Help me wash Jasper. Please?" She batted her eyelashes at him, and he just shook his head, determined not to give in to that all-too-cute and damn sexy look of hers.

Liam glanced at Jasper and held back a laugh. The first time he'd met the all-white Husky, the dog's face had been stained blue. Today was even better.

"Your dog is green."

"Yes. Yes, he is. But he's shy about it, so don't look at him with pity in your eyes."

Liam blinked, then looked down at Jasper, who was rolling around on the grass in Arden's back yard rather than paying attention to them.

"Shy?"

"Dogs can be shy, Liam Montgomery."

"Sure. But not your dog. Your dog is never shy."

"He can be." She raised her chin, and Liam held back a laugh.

"Sure, baby." Then he leaned down and kissed the tip of her nose. When she glared, he winced. "Babe."

"Don't *babe* me. Jasper can be shy. But that's not the point. He needs a bath. You wanted to go on a date, and I said I needed to do this first. So, here we are."

"I'll help, I'll help." Liam raised his hands in surrender. "But I still want to know how he's green. Did he throw his whole body into a vat of green frosting?"

When her lips quirked into a smile, he leaned down and kissed her again. He couldn't help it. He *liked* kissing her. He should probably stop, probably take a step back and not act so domesticated and as if he had a place in her home like this, but he couldn't seem to quit.

This was...it was nice. And he didn't want to stop.

She moaned into him and then pulled away, pointing the end of the hose at him. "Hey there, Montgomery. Don't get all swoony on me."

"Swoony? I think *you* were the one that moaned. You're the swoony one." He honestly couldn't believe he was having this conversation, but he couldn't help it. Arden was fun, his distraction. Exactly what he needed.

"We're getting off-topic," she said quickly, her hand on

the handle of the nozzle. "Jasper is green because he likes freshly mowed grass. So much so, as you can see, he *has* to roll around in it."

"You mowed the lawn? I told you'd I'd handle it if Cross couldn't." He didn't want her to tire herself out. They'd already talked about this.

She narrowed her eyes. "I can do this small patch, thank you very much. We're *not* getting into that. Anyway, my baby boy loves grass, but...he's a white dog. White fur plus newly cut grass equals a green dog. So, he needs a bath." She fluttered those lashes again. "And I could use your help."

She held out the hose, and he grinned. "Not going to spray me down?"

"Oh, I could. But that'll be for later. First, though, we have to catch Jasper."

"Catch?" Jasper was one of the most well-behaved dogs he knew, so the idea of having to catch him didn't make much sense.

"He doesn't like b-a-t-h-s out here. The diva would rather go to the doggie spa," she whispered as she leaned toward him.

"Why are you whispering?" Liam whispered back.

"He knows." As if on cue, Jasper stopped rolling around, and his ears perked.

"Uh-oh," Liam said, smiling.

"Get the bucket filled," Arden called as she started

chasing after Jasper, laughter in her voice. "There's already soap!"

Liam just shook his head and did as he was told, laughing so hard now his stomach hurt as he watched Arden and Jasper chase *each other* around the yard. He was about to join her but, right at that moment, Jasper decided he wanted water of all things and leapt into the bucket.

Soapy water sloshed over the sides and high into the air, landing on the grass as well as Liam's entire body, though mostly his face.

Arden's laughter cut off, and he wiped the soap from his eyes before looking at her. She had her hand over her mouth, her face red as she tried not to laugh.

"Your dog, Arden. Your dog."

"He's shy!"

"Lies. All lies."

Soon, they were both covered in soapy water and dog kisses. Jasper stood still enough to be scrubbed down since all Arden had to do was ask. Apparently, the chasing was all part of the game the two loved, and Liam wasn't going to complain. After all, he had his own quirks. Arden's just seemed to revolve around her dog.

By the time Jasper was partially dry and sunning himself on the patio, Liam was exhausted and drenched.

"I can't believe you do that on your own," he said, still laughing.

"Oh, my brothers usually help, or I call the groomer. Like I said, he loves that for some reason." She shrugged, and Liam raised his brows. "I thought this would be a nice home date or something. I sort of suck at being romantic."

Something clenched in his belly at that, but he pushed it to the side. "Oh?"

"Yeah, not the best idea, but your shirt is wet and stuck to your very sexy chest, so I think I'm winning."

Liam gave a pointed look to her pale peach shirt and her *very* thin bra with the outline of her nipples.

"Yeah, pretty sure *I'm* the winner here."

Her nipples pebbled under his gaze, and he swallowed hard, adjusting himself under his wet jeans. That was probably going to leave a mark.

"Don't look at me like that," she whispered, her hands moving to cover her breasts.

"I don't know, kind of hard to stop with you looking all sexy and cute like that."

"Oh?" she asked, wiping a stray bubble from her cheek.

"Yeah, *oh.*" He took a few steps toward her and cupped her face. "Hey."

"Hey," she breathed. "Thanks for your help."

"Any time, babe." He leaned down, brushing his lips along hers. "Anytime."

And that was the truth. He'd actually had fun, and he

couldn't fight this pull towards her, this attraction. Arden made him smile, made him laugh.

And considering everything that had been going on recently, she seemed to be precisely what he needed.

He'd think about what that meant later. For now?

For now, he had a wet and soapy Arden in his hands. What more did he need?

CHAPTER 12

"**Y**ou know I have no idea what's going on, right?" Arden asked, and Liam just snorted.

He wrapped his arm around her shoulders and brought her closer to him, away from the other guys also seated at the bar.

"I thought you knew basketball," Liam said before kissing the top of her head.

"Oh, I know basketball. As in I've been to a Denver Nuggets game or two. But I don't actually know college ball."

The guys behind her sneered, laughing to themselves as they whispered. Liam glared. He was bigger than both of them, also older, but fuck them and the high horse they rode in on.

"You probably shouldn't scream that while we're at a

bar watching March Madness," Liam said and then kissed her forehead. He kept kissing her. Couldn't stop it. All he wanted to do was keep his mouth on her, but he knew that it was a compulsion, though one he could get used to. She was his distraction, his addiction. And that was fine. He had a feeling he was hers, as well. At least, he hoped he was. Her addiction anyway. Her distraction? He had to wonder if he was helping with that at all. But he wasn't going to worry too much about it. Tonight was their sixth date—seventh if he counted the coffee date they had. And he would count it, mostly so he wouldn't actually think that he had slept with Arden on their first date. Not that that was a bad thing, but he had a feeling she wasn't too thrilled about that idea. So, their seventh date it was. However, now that they were sitting in a bar surrounded by a bunch of men and women who just wanted to watch college basketball, he had to wonder if he had made a mistake by coming here.

"We could go," Liam said quickly. "It's not the end of the world."

She just rolled her eyes and kissed his chin. Then she leaned forward and took a sip of her Manhattan. Most people were drinking beers or martinis. They were having a sale or a special on vodka and whiskey that night, probably to get rid of some of the well. That was fine with Liam. He'd have his single beer, but with hard liquor on the table with a lot of the people, he knew they couldn't stay for the whole night. March Madness got rowdy as it was. You didn't need to add liquor to that fire.

"I'm having fun. I just wanted to let you know that I don't actually know the teams beyond like who Duke is."

"We don't talk about Duke," Liam said deadpan, and the guys at his side laughed.

"Duke sucks," one of the guys shouted.

"Duke sucks!" The bar erupted, and Arden closed her eyes. "I see. Apparently, Duke sucks. Good to know. Cheers." She held up her Manhattan and took another drink. Liam just smiled, taking a sip of his beer.

"Well, I could help you with the whole idea of March Madness if that helps, but I don't want to mansplain anything to you."

She chuffed, shaking her head. "You don't mansplain. My brothers? *They* mansplain. Or rather they big-brother-splain. I don't know if they actually do that to other women. Mostly just me."

"Well, I'm pretty sure I do the same to Bristol, so it might be a brother thing."

"And a male thing. But that's fine. I know about brackets, I just don't know the back stories behind every single team to be able to pick who I want. Plus, it's not like I know who's supposed to be the Cinderella team or not."

"The Cinderella team isn't just randomly picked and doesn't always happen," he said gently.

"Well, it should. It's always a nice story."

"It's sort of *why* it's the story. This year, though? It's playing out like usual. The lower-seeded teams advancing."

And then he tapped his knuckles on the bar, aware that anyone listening was grinning at him.

"Sorry, I probably shouldn't have said that."

"Oh, I know all about jinxes and all that. I do watch football and hockey. I just watch more of the professional stuff, not the collegiate level. But I'm learning." She held up her hands and looked around at the patrons of the bar that were somewhat paying attention to them now. "I promise. I'm learning. Just tell me who to root for, and I'll do better research next time."

The guys lifted their glasses in cheers, and she grinned.

Well, it seemed his Arden had a way with people. She'd already won them over. Just like she'd won him over. They sat at the bar for a bit longer, finishing up their shared wings and dip. Arden had one Manhattan and then switched to club soda with lime. He only had his one beer, and then joined her with the club soda. But when things got a little rowdy as the crowd favorite started to lose, Liam kept looking around, making sure Arden was safe.

It shouldn't have been this loud. But, apparently, one

of the local fraternities had shown up, and it was getting a bit out of hand.

They would have to leave soon, but from the way Arden kept wincing, he had a feeling it was going to be now.

"You okay?"

She nodded and then rubbed her arm. "I'm fine. Just people knocking into the back of us. I think I'm going to end up with some bruises."

He narrowed his eyes, fisting his hands on the bar. "What the fuck?"

"I'm *fine*. It's just…I think I'm about to flare, so I'm bruising a little easier than normal. I'm fine."

He swallowed hard, trying not to remember how in pain she had looked at the hospital when she'd had her last flare. He didn't know enough about lupus. Didn't know how to help. Didn't know if he *could* help, and he was afraid that he couldn't. But they could at least get out of there. "Let's go."

She grimaced, rubbing her stomach. "Yeah. I'm not feeling too well. I'm sorry. I hate this."

He shook his head, nodded at the bartender as he left money for the rest of their bill on the counter, and then helped Arden off the barstool.

"Come on, let's go get you tucked into bed."

"I'm sorry," she repeated. And then she said it again. And again. Even as they were driving towards her house, she just kept apologizing. But she was groaning, holding herself, and he was getting worried.

"Arden. Don't be sorry. Do I need to take you to the hospital?"

He got off the highway and kept shooting glances at her, getting more worried by the minute.

"It's just life. It's not too bad." She grimaced then, and he cursed.

"Not too bad? Look at you, Arden. You can barely sit up in the seat."

"I know. But this isn't too bad. Really. It's been worse. I probably shouldn't have had the whiskey. Or the wings. And that just sucks. But don't worry, I didn't know I shouldn't have had the liquor or the spicy food until I had it. It's not like I can tell when something's going to make my body freak out. If I did, I would avoid it all. Or at least try to. But, yeah, I think I'm about to flare, so I'm just going to go home. Okay? I'm so sorry we had to cut the night short."

"Don't be sorry." His hands tightened on the steering wheel as he pulled into her driveway. "It's not your fucking fault."

"Yeah, but I mean…we're still going home, aren't we?"

He sighed, turned off the engine, and then got out of the car. Before he could go and help her out, she was already wobbling out on her own and pushed him away as he tried to help.

"For fuck's sake, Arden, just let me help." He knew he was acting irrationally, but he felt so helpless. He couldn't help. And the way she kept pushing him away annoyed the fuck out of him.

"I've got it, Liam. I always do."

"You don't have to do everything on your own, Arden."

She opened the door as Jasper came out and rubbed his nose on her palm. She looked over her shoulder and gave Liam a sad smile. "I've gotten pretty good at it, Liam. Thanks for the date tonight. Sorry lupus struck again. I'll see you later?"

He gave her a tight nod, but he didn't kiss her. He was afraid that even his touch would hurt her. He couldn't let himself do that. Couldn't allow himself to do anything except just walk away as she closed the door, taking herself and her dog away from him.

She was hurting, and it was something that he couldn't fix. He was afraid he'd never be able to figure out how to help her.

And he didn't know what to do about that. Didn't know why his gut felt like he was making the wrong choice. That he was making another mistake.

But he didn't have the answers, so he got into his car and slowly rolled out of the driveway, wondering the entire time what exactly to do about Arden.

CHAPTER 13

*L*iam promised himself that he wasn't going to murder his hero, but if Nash didn't get back on outline and do what he was supposed to do, Liam would have to start a whole new series because he would kill every single person in the current one.

Seriously, he might just burn his hero in effigy.

Or maybe he would kill off Nash and just write Penny's story. Penny was being silent, wasn't doing anything, and that probably should have worried him. But since Nash was being such an idiot in his brain, Penny was a cool drink of water, a nice slice of relief in the hell that was Liam's mind, even if she wasn't being very active.

Yeah, he had conversations with his characters in his head. So did every other writer he knew. Even the highly analytical ones who did everything by the book and adhered to outline and had character profiles where it was just pieces of data in a spreadsheet. They talked to their characters, even if they didn't admit it.

They couldn't put the words to paper without them being filled in in their minds first.

Or Liam was just losing *his* mind and procrastinating by worrying about the craft of writing rather than writing the book itself.

His character was currently hiding behind a boulder as gunfire erupted, and a bomb went off, but instead of being concerned about what needed to happen next, Nash was worried about Penny. Not because Penny was in danger. No, Penny was just fine. She just wasn't talking to Nash, just like she wasn't talking to Liam.

Instead, she had pushed Nash away and was walking away from everything, saying that she could do everything on her own and didn't need anyone else.

Yeah, Liam didn't need a degree in psychology or even a therapy session to realize that he was literally putting his own life into this book.

It had been four days since he had seen Arden in person, and he didn't know what to think about that. Yeah, most of that was because he was on deadline and actually working, and it wasn't like the two of them saw each other every day. But even their texts were few and far between, and she had said that she'd been sleepy more often than not.

That concerned him. Hell, everything to do with Arden worried him these days.

When he wasn't working on his book, trying to throw himself into Nash and Penny's world, he was looking up everything he could about lupus.

Arden had given him the gist of it, but he had watched YouTube videos of firsthand accounts describing what they were going through. He had read article after article about misdiagnoses and exactly what killed people with lupus, and how the symptoms sometimes masked themselves as other things, and how most people ended up with more than one type of disease.

How the hell had Arden survived this for her entire life? How did she skip around and smile and act like nothing was wrong? Most of the time, she looked like she was fine, that she wasn't sick.

But she was, and he didn't know how to help her. The fact that he was putting this all on himself? Turning her disease around so it made him think about how he felt? That made him feel like a fucking asshole.

But he hated that he couldn't help her. Though maybe he could. Perhaps he could at least make things easier for her.

She would just have to let him in so he could.

That meant he needed to be willing to take the next step.

Because Arden was only supposed to be a distraction.

He had told himself that over and over again. And yet, even though it was true, and he was thinking about her and not the other shit in his life outside of his work, she wasn't just a distraction anymore. And he didn't know how he felt about that.

Hence why Nash and Penny were giving him fits in his book.

It was hard to jump into his own world of fiction and pretend that everything was fine and that he knew what he was doing when it wasn't fine. Nothing was okay.

He tried to write another hundred words, and then a page, and then he just quit. He had a feeling he was going to delete the last chapter he had written. None of it was salvageable.

He didn't know where Nash was going, and that worried him just as much as his own path worried him. Because he had plotted Nash's story, he knew what needed to happen and what would come of it. He just didn't know exactly what would happen at the end. Because he was at the precipice of something, a fork in the road regarding where Nash could go.

Liam hadn't made that decision yet.

He'd have to soon.

But not today.

Instead, he sat back from his computer and pulled out his phone.

He didn't know if Arden was working today, though he knew she pretty much worked every day, just maybe not for a full eight hours if she wasn't up to it.

But he wanted to video chat with her. He hadn't seen her face, and he wanted to see her. It just worried him that maybe she didn't want to see *him*.

"Get your head out of your ass and just call her." He said the words to himself, but he knew he was losing his mind. At least when it came to Arden. And his family. And his work.

Oh, good, it seemed he had everything settled in front of him. Or nothing. Whatever.

He pressed Arden's name on his call list, and waited for the phone to connect, looking at his own face in the screen as he waited for her to answer. He squinted, figuring that he probably should have shaved or at least washed his face so he didn't look like someone on deadline or a person having a really shitty day. But...too late.

Arden answered, and he could tell that she was in her bedroom, her head nestled on her pillow. The dark circles under her eyes were more vivid than he'd ever seen them.

"Did I wake you?" he asked, his voice low.

Arden tried to smile, but he noticed that it didn't reach her eyes. Damn it. "No, I'm just lying down. Me and Jasper." She moved the phone so it showed the front of her body under the blanket and Jasper nestled against her side, his big head nuzzled right under her breasts. The dog looked at the phone, and Liam swore he could see a pleading look in Jasper's eyes. Begging for help? Or to go back to bed?

Liam couldn't even read Arden's face, how was he supposed to read her dog's?

"So, you're awake? Looks like you're playing hooky and sleeping," he said, trying to tease. Just attempting to make her smile. When had his life's mission become making Arden smile? He didn't know, but he was damn well going to find out. And he sure as shit was going to make her smile.

"I've been working all day. My stuff's actually on the other side of me in bed. Today was a work-in-bed day. Not the best for my body, but not the worst, either. I just got back from letting Jasper out into the back yard, and now he's just hanging out with me in bed. Because he's a good doggo, isn't he?" She sing-songed the last part, and Liam watched her arm move. He figured she was petting Jasper's head.

"Has he gone out for a W-A-L-K?" he asked, holding back a smile at the fact that he spelled it out just like she did.

Her eyes widened, and she shook her head. "No, not yet. But we can't spell out the word either. He's learned what it means."

Liam snorted but nodded.

"Is there anything I can do for you?"

"I'm okay. Feeling better. I know it doesn't look it, but I am. We're just hanging out here. How's the book going? Or is that something I shouldn't ask?"

Liam leaned back in the chair and groaned. "Let's not talk about the book. Ever."

"That bad?" she asked, snuggling into the pillow.

"Well, I'm at the part of the process where I hate everything I've ever written in my life, and I wonder why I even decided on this as a job. Maybe I should find a new one. I mean, I've already had one career. This is my second. Why not a third?"

"If you do not finish this so I can find out what happens with Nash and Penny, I'm going to be very disappointed in you, Liam Montgomery."

Liam just smiled, looking at her drawn face, and wishing he was there to try and make her better. Or at least try to make her *feel* better.

"Okay, I will work on writing this for you. But only for you."

"That makes me feel special."

He swallowed hard, looking at her face, wishing he was there with her.

"You are special."

Then he leaned forward, frowning. The light had

moved in the room, and now whatever sun was coming through her windows was on her face.

"Is that a bruise on your jaw?"

She winced. "Yeah, I was trying to put on my shirt, and I hit myself in the face. I know, I'm a dork. But, yeah, I'm bruising."

"Your face looks a bit yellow, too," Liam said, worried. "Seriously, when the natural light hits you, you look kind of yellow."

She sighed and nodded. "Yeah, I think it's just the flareup. But I'm going to call my doctor later. I thought so earlier, too, but I tend to overreact sometimes. But if you see it? I'll call the doc."

"Arden. I'll be right over."

"No, finish your work. At least, what you need to do for today. I've got this. It's just life, Liam. I'll deal." She sighed. "I've got to go. Need to pay for that medical insurance and all." She winked, and Liam growled.

"Arden."

"If you can't laugh at what's trying to kick you down, then what's the point? I'm fine. I've been through this before. I really do need to go, though. Okay? I'll talk to you later."

"I'll talk to you later, too." They hung up, and Liam looked down at his phone, squeezing it so tightly he was surprised that the glass didn't shatter.

"Fuck."

He didn't throw his phone, but he did set it down hard, pissed off.

There was nothing he could do. Literally nothing. He couldn't do anything about Arden. About the book. There was nothing he could do about his family. He was a man who did things. He had a goal and then set his mind to it and did it. If his siblings needed something, he did it. Before everything had changed, if his parents needed something, he did it.

Now? He wasn't doing anything. He was wallowing, and he hated it. He needed to make a decision. He needed to figure out what the fuck he wanted to do. But all he could do right now was think about Arden and see her face, that bruise, and the pallor of her skin.

He couldn't fix it.

But maybe he could help her feel better.

He just needed to stay out of her way while he did so.

But before he could think more about that, his doorbell rang. He frowned. The only person he wanted to see right then was Arden, and he knew for a fact that it wasn't her. There was no way she would have made it all the way over to his house by then, and he had a feeling she wanted to hide how she was feeling from him anyway. Because why would she want to lean on someone when she had herself?

And because that sounded a little bit too much like *his*

attitude, he went to the door and pulled it open quickly without looking.

"Oh," he said, the breath virtually knocked out of him.

"Oh." Timothy Montgomery, the man Liam had called *"Father"* all his life, pinched the bridge of his nose and then shoved past Liam into the house.

"Why don't you come on in? Sure, make yourself at home."

"You know what? You can stop with the attitude."

"Seriously? This is my house."

"And I'm your father."

"No, you're not? Didn't we already learn that?"

"Oh, grow the fuck up, Liam." Timothy started pacing around the living room, and Liam just stood there, shocked. They yelled at each other, but not like this. Usually not with so much emotion. Generally, it was to let off some steam, and there was normally something beneath it that said they would always be there for each other.

But that had shattered. It wasn't there right then.

Liam couldn't even catch his breath.

"I love your mother. I have always loved her. And I love you, Liam."

"I just..." Liam let his voice trail off, not sure what to say.

"I know this is confusing. And I know we should have found a way to tell you. We just didn't know how. You have always been mine. Even when we weren't a hundred percent sure that we were going to get the paternal rights signed over to us, you were mine. The only reason I'm not on your original birth certificate is because we weren't sure of the legalities of that. And, honestly, we weren't sure what Steve was going to do. He signed his rights away, and that's on him. It's not on you. You were always wanted. By your mother. By me. By everyone else in this family."

"It's just hard to think about. Don't you get that? It's just hard to get through it all and not be angry."

"You have every right to be angry. You can be mad that we lied. You can be upset that we withheld it from you. But you know we didn't do it to hurt you. We did it because we didn't want to hurt you."

"Really?"

"Of course, really. You are my son. I held you the day you were born. I was always there for you. Even when you were a little dick when you were a model, or when you were a teenager and stole the car so you could go on a date with that girl named Mindy."

"Her name was Maxie," Liam corrected, smiling at that.

"Mindy, Maxie, it doesn't matter. You disobeyed us, and you stole the car. And then it was something that Ethan and Aaron and even Bristol tried to do because their big brother Liam did it."

"Don't know why. I was grounded for like two months."

"But their awesome big brother did it, so they needed to try it, too. They have always looked up to you, Liam. They are your siblings. They are your family. They are blood." Timothy ran his hands over his face and turned away. When his voice cracked, Liam swallowed hard, not knowing what to do or say.

"I know I'm not blood. I know that I'm not your biological father. My sperm wasn't part of this."

"Really?" Liam said with a snort.

"What? If you want to talk about how Steve is related to you, it is that clinical. His sperm fertilized an egg. That is the only part of him that is you. I see nothing of him in you. I see your mother. I see your grandparents. I see your siblings. And I even see me, goddammit. I see me in the way you act, in the way you laugh. In how you throw yourself into everything you do. I don't know what's going to happen next, but I love you. You are my son. You're a Montgomery. I raised you. Don't turn away because we were fools." A tear fell down his face, and Timothy wiped his cheek.

"I don't know what else to say. Just don't let this break us. We're Montgomerys. We're strong. We never give up. We never give up on each other. Don't let this break us."

"I don't know, Dad."

His dad's eyes widened, and he swallowed hard. "You haven't used that word since you found out. *Dad.*"

"The whole idea that it is just genetics, I get. And I'm never going to come to terms with everything all at once. I'm not that person. I never have been. But I thought I was a Montgomery," Liam said, his voice hollow.

"You are."

"Then why the lies? I think...I think that's what hurts the most. The lies."

"I told you, we were fools. We thought we knew best. We were wrong. But just know that I love you. Your mother loves you. Your family loves you. When you're through processing whatever you're going through in your head, we'll be there. Your mother will be there."

"I don't hate her," Liam said quickly. "I don't blame her for what happened, just what happened after." His father's shoulders sagged a bit. Timothy nodded. "Be sure you let her know that whenever you actually talk to her again. Or any of us. I hate seeing my wife like this, Liam. I hate seeing your mom like she is right now. And I know we deserve a little bit of it. But we've always been there for you. And we always want to be. So...I'm going now. I just figured I'd barge my way in like any good Montgomery would do and tell you that I love you. If you need to hit me or yell at me or do something else, do it. Just don't do it to your mom. She's been through enough. Don't let this break us."

Liam nodded but didn't say anything. He couldn't.

When his dad left, Liam just stood there, looking down at his fists.

He didn't blame anyone for how he'd been born. That wasn't what upset him. It wasn't like his mom had cheated. Even if she had, he hadn't been a part of that. That was between his mom and his dad.

For all he knew, his dad had slept with a bunch of women when they were on their break.

That wasn't the problem. It was the lies.

Sure, they had apologized. At least those Liam had let apologize.

He needed to figure it all out. But he needed time.

Maybe then he'd stop acting like an asshole.

His office phone rang, and he cursed. It seemed like he was never going to have even a few moments to himself so he could think.

Of course, everything happening all at once helped him to not actually deal with any of his problems.

As a writer, he kind of liked that.

It was his agent's name on the caller ID of his phone, and he answered, a little weary.

"Yes?"

"Hey, Liam. Just reading over the chapters. I think I figured out something that can help."

"How do you always know when I'm having issues?" Liam growled.

"Because we've been working together for years, and I know everything."

"Yeah, right."

"Ah, shut up. But I really think you need to add more about Nash's family. That might help. Right? If you add more about where Nash came from, it might help you figure out where he needs to go."

His agent talked for a bit more, and Liam just grumbled and nodded, even though his agent couldn't see him.

When they hung up, Liam looked down at his phone and just shook his head.

Family. It always came back to family. Because how could you go and look forward when you couldn't figure out where you came from.

Well, fuck. It seemed Liam wouldn't be able to run from his problems. But that didn't mean he had to think about them right then.

Instead, he put his phone into his pocket and grabbed his keys. He was going to make sure Arden was okay. He would at least do one thing right when everything else he was doing felt wrong.

Because Arden needed him.

Even if she wouldn't admit it.

Maybe if he could at least fix one thing, he wouldn't have to fix the rest.

At least, not right then.

CHAPTER 14

*A*rden slowly made her way to the door, her feet shuffling along the carpet as Jasper pressed into her thigh, helping her stand.

It wasn't that he was an actual emotional support dog or a therapy dog, but he was just so loving and helpful that he automatically helped her when she needed it. She knew she should probably get him more training to help her when things got truly bad, but she couldn't think about that right then. Her mind was a little too fuzzy to think about anything. She didn't even have the energy to open the door fully or look through the peephole. So she opened it a crack and leaned her head against the cool wood of the door, trying to catch her breath. "Liam," she whispered, her lips dry.

"Arden, baby. Dear God." He pushed his way inside

and put his hands on her hips, keeping her steady. Jasper didn't even growl. Instead, he leaned against her tightly, looking up at Liam as if her dog needed help, too.

She couldn't even take care of her dog right then.

Something was wrong, terribly wrong.

She just hurt. Everywhere.

Liam moved one hand up her side to cup her face and then put his thumb on her cheek so he could look into Arden's eyes. She might have thought it was weird, but everything felt strange just then.

"What's wrong? Arden?"

"I don't feel good."

"No, shit."

"I was trying to get ahold of my brothers, but maybe I'll just call Uber. I don't know."

It sounded like she was in a tunnel. "I think I just need to sleep." She knew she wasn't making any sense, and when she found herself leaning heavily into Liam's side, she heard him curse under his breath. "An Uber?"

"I need to go to the ER. And I can't get ahold of my family. Uber or something can get me there. I just don't want to call an ambulance. I'm not there yet."

"Are you fucking kidding me? No. I'm taking you. Come on, let's get to the ER."

"No. I don't want to take your time away. You're busy and on deadline. And you weren't supposed to be here."

Her eyes weren't even open, and she was leaning

into him even more, the feel of his hand running up and down her back actually painful. She moved away from him, wincing. He narrowed his eyes as she opened hers.

"Am I hurting you?"

"My skin hurts. My hair hurts. Everything hurts."

Liam searched her face, and he gave her a tight nod. "Okay. You're going to shut up. I'm here. I'm going to take you to the ER. There will be no calling a rideshare service. Nothing like that. And if your brothers aren't answering, and they are as overprotective as you say? That means they're just not near their phones at the moment. Because I know they would be here faster than you could call the next brother if they could. They're likely just like me when it comes to Bristol. So, I'm here. And you're going to have to deal with that. We've slept together. That means we're at least sort of friends at this point. More than friends."

"I'm so glad that we have a label now," she said, fading.

"We don't. But come on. We're going to get you to the hospital. Do you have your purse?" She nodded. "Good. Jasper okay here by himself for a bit?"

"Yeah, I'll text my brothers." She knew she barely whispered the words, and he cursed again before lifting her into his arms.

She let out a gasp, and Jasper barked once but didn't do it again. Apparently, her dog trusted Liam. That was good because she wasn't sure of anything right now. Everything hurt. Everything.

She drifted in and out as Liam got her into his car and buckled her in, setting her purse on the floor.

Then he went back to the front door of the house, and she heard him saying something to Jasper before he left and locked the door behind him. She blinked, and then he was in the car next to her, pulling out of the driveway.

"University Hospital the one you want?" he asked. His voice low.

"Yeah, they know me there."

"I am not going to really talk about that. Because I'll probably get angry. But I'm going to text Bristol when we get there and get you settled. That way, she can come and take care of Jasper if you or she can't get ahold of your brothers. I'm going to need your key for that, though. You okay with that?"

Arden leaned her head against the window and nodded. "As long as Jasper's fine. I don't care. I'm just tired."

"Okay, then. We'll get him taken care of. I promise you. And you'll be fine."

They sent her back through the waiting room doors quickly and to a bed with an intravenous IV. She didn't even have to wait. Apparently, the yellow tone of her skin and eyes had scared the nurses enough to hurry things along. To be honest, it scared her, too. Her stomach ached, and her whole body shook, but she wasn't alone.

Liam was there. Had been the whole damn time.

Even when the nurse looked at Arden and asked if she wanted Liam out of the room, mostly because Liam wasn't her husband or brother or anyone related to her, Liam had simply stood there, unmoving. Yeah, he would have left if he'd been forced to, but she hadn't wanted him to go. She didn't want to be alone.

Maybe that made her weak. But, damn it, she already felt weak enough.

What more did she need?

Hours. It took hours, and yet he stayed. Her brothers came, but Liam was always there.

"We're going to admit you, Miss Brady. You just keep holding on, and we'll get you what you need. We're glad you got here when you did. Lupus is a very serious disease."

"She knows that." Liam growled. "Believe me. She knows that." Arden smiled and reached out to pat his hand. She couldn't really do much more than move her fingers a bit because her whole body was shaking, but she was glad that he was there. Even if it was embarrassing.

Because not only did she have the shakes, and her body was utterly yellow, her stomach also hurt, and she was having digestion issues. Her body seriously did not want to be here right now. Nor did it want Liam to stay.

She was pretty sure her system was revolting and never wanted her to be in a serious relationship. Ever. But while most men would have already left, Liam hadn't. He stayed. The whole damn time. Even when they moved her to her own room and hooked her up to her new drugs that would stabilize her AST and ALT levels, Liam stayed.

She was worried that she might come to rely on that. And she couldn't.

Because what would happen when he left? What would happen when this got to be too much? Because while this was bad, she'd actually had worse.

And people couldn't stay all the time.

"You want another ice chip?" Liam asked, giving her hand a gentle squeeze.

"I'm okay. I'm sorry," Arden said quickly, lowering her gaze. "I'm just sorry that you're here."

"I'm not." He frowned down at her, even as he leaned closer. "Well, I'm sorry that you're here. I'm sorry that you're in so much pain and that your body is being a son of a bitch right now." That made her smile. "But I'm not going anywhere. I'm right here."

"Yeah, you are. For now. But this is my life, Liam. This happens sometimes. This is sort of what I'm used to. You shouldn't have to deal with this. Maybe you should just go."

Liam stood up then, keeping his hand on hers as he

hovered over her body and narrowed his eyes. "No. Others may have left. I'm not." That made her flinch, and she closed her eyes, sucking in a deep breath.

"I'm sorry. But that's the truth. I'm not leaving. And I know others in your life left, you told me that. And I get it. Sometimes, things are hard. But I'm here."

"It was easier for others to go before," she began, licking her dry lips. She felt better, much better than she had before, but she still just wanted to get this over with. She did not want it to hurt anymore. Not only her body but also her soul.

"What do you mean?" he asked.

"I have friends, you know. A lot of friends. Or at least a good circle. But I kept having to say no to dinners and going out. They all went to Disney once, and I had to say no because I wasn't feeling well. Because I knew if I was out in the sun for four days in July in Florida, I would feel like crap, and it would be worse coming home. I had to say no to birthdays because I wasn't feeling well. Or if I went when I wasn't feeling well, people got a little sad or annoyed that I was quiet in the corner. That I wasn't being my normal, peppy self. I'm not always sick. Well, that's not true. I am, and I will always be sick. But I don't always have symptoms. And that's the difference. Nine times out of ten? I feel okay. Like there's nothing wrong except some aches. I feel like I could run a half marathon. Okay, maybe not. Maybe just down the block." She smiled, and Liam grinned, even though it didn't quite reach his eyes all the way.

"And then they left?" he asked softly.

"Yeah, they did. It just... After a while, they stopped asking me to things. Why would they keep doing it if I was just going to say no? Some people moved on, some moved away. Those all started families and got married and had entire lives of their own. It was easy not to look back and think of me. Even Josh." Arden swallowed hard.

Liam glared. "Josh?"

"My ex. We were pretty serious for a while. At least, I thought we were. But he didn't want *a broken bird*, as he called it."

"Where is he, and can I kick his ass?" Liam growled.

"No need. My brothers tried to already, but then I pulled them away."

"Why did you do that?"

"Because I don't want anyone going to jail for me. But, Liam? It's hard to be my friend. Or whatever we are since we're not actually doing labels." He didn't laugh. "It's tough."

"Life's fucking hard. Friendships are difficult. And I don't know what we are to each other. Because that's not something we've talked about yet. And it's not something we're going to talk about right now because you're in a hospital bed, and I'm pissed off. So, yeah, life is hard, but I'm not going anywhere."

"But you have to work." Now she was grasping at straws. "But, seriously."

"Seriously, I can write the damn book sitting next to you."

"But my brothers will be here. You don't have to stay."

"I feel like you're pushing me away. And I don't like it. You don't want me here because you are just fine without me and you're kind of tired of me? That's one thing. But you pushing me away because you're afraid I'm going to walk away? I don't like that. And so what if your brothers will be here? Fine. I'll be here, too. All of us will be. We'll deal with each other, and we'll make you laugh. And then when you go home, we'll make sure you're settled there, too. I'm not going anywhere."

Arden's jaw tightened, and she wondered what she was feeling. Because she wasn't sure if this all meant that Liam wanted more with her. Or was he running from something?

By the way he was acting, given how they had been very careful not to talk about what that major thing in his life was, she was really afraid this wasn't just about her.

"What are you running from?" she whispered. He sighed.

Well, then.

It wasn't just her.

"I want to be here. But, yeah, I guess since you're here,

and I am too, I suppose there're a few things I should tell you."

"Okay. If you're here, and I'm here, too."

She hoped she didn't break in the process of him telling her.

CHAPTER 15

Liam leaned back in the chair just for a moment before giving Arden's hand a squeeze and then standing up. Not only to stretch his back after sitting in that chair for hours now but because he needed to think. He might as well tell her. Might as well get her mind off what was going on with her. Plus, he *wanted* to tell her. He needed to. Even though he didn't know what that meant.

Because the fact that he needed to talk to her just told him that maybe she wasn't only a distraction.

Hell, he was sitting by her side while she was in a hospital bed, worried as fuck that something else could go wrong, or that she wouldn't make it. Or would be in so much pain, that he wouldn't be able to do anything. As it was, he couldn't do anything.

He hated seeing Arden in pain.

And he knew this wasn't a distraction. *She* wasn't a distraction.

So, he was going to tell her. Because he had to. Because he wanted to.

"Do you remember the first time we met?" he asked, trying to figure out where to start. Might as well start at the beginning.

"Yes," she said cautiously. "I mean, it was pretty similar to where we are now."

"Yeah." He let out a rough chuckle. "I really wish it wasn't so similar."

"At least you're not in a hospital bed," she said, trying to sound a little happier, more energetic than she probably was, at least that's what he figured from the tone of her voice.

"You don't have to be brave with me," he whispered. "And I'd rather it be me in that bed than you. Any day of the week. I'd rather it be me."

Tears filled her eyes, and she blinked them away, so he leaned over and ran his thumb over her cheek, careful not to touch her too hard. He didn't know how her skin felt today. For all he knew, just the barest brush would hurt her. But she didn't flinch. Instead, she smiled and leaned into his touch ever so slightly.

"If I'm honest, I'd rather it be neither of us. But don't worry, Liam. I've been here before. I can handle it."

"You shouldn't have to handle it," he growled and stood up again, needing to pace. "But I'm getting off track," he said and then let out a sigh.

"Okay. Talk to me."

She was too good for him. That much he knew. But he didn't have time to think about that. Didn't want to think about it just yet. "Okay, where was I?"

"Our first meeting."

"Yeah, in the hospital. So, when we got home after that, my family was all at my house, and it turned out that we needed some paperwork or something. I don't really know the details, and I think Ethan actually took care of everything for me."

Liam pinched the bridge of his nose. "Yeah, my brother took care of it for me. Because he's good like that. Because I've had my head so far up my ass recently, I couldn't even take care of my own medical shit."

"My brothers take care of things for me, too. Sometimes, I just have to sign. But I let them. Because I trust them."

It felt like a dagger to the heart, and he swallowed hard. "Yeah, I trust Ethan. And Bristol. And Aaron." He rubbed his jaw. "And up until that day, I trusted my parents, too."

Her eyes widened. "What happened?"

He was just going to blurt it out because, hell, this lead-up was killing him. "Well, I needed a birth certificate for something. And, apparently, the man I thought was my father my entire life that made me a Montgomery? Yeah, not so much. Not my father. Instead, it was some guy named Steve."

Liam told her the whole story about the breakup, but she didn't laugh at the *Friends* joke. But then again, neither had he. It hadn't been funny before, and it wasn't now. Maybe one day. He just didn't know when. He told her how he'd been acting, how he hadn't talked to his mother since he got the news. And how his dad had shown up at his place. *His dad.*

Yeah, Timothy was his dad. That wasn't the part that hurt. It was the lying. And when he said that, Arden reached out her hand. He took her palm, giving her fingers a gentle squeeze. He didn't want to hurt her. But he had a feeling he was going to anyway. That's what he'd been doing recently, after all. Right? Hurting those he cared about.

"I'm so sorry. That's just…that's insane, Liam."

"I know, right?" He let out another chuckle and then sat down in the chair beside her bed so he could keep his hand on hers.

"So, that's why you didn't call. Right?" She looked like she was embarrassed for asking, so Liam was truthful. "Yeah. I would have called." He paused. "I liked you in that hospital bed—that's not what I meant," he said quickly as her eyes widened. He shook his head. He was fumbling this. "I meant, I liked you when I met you. I didn't like the fact that you were in a hospital bed. Hell, for a man who uses words for a living, I'm not doing very well today."

"Well, I don't think you're supposed to when something like that makes you go off-kilter. At least, not in my experience. When I'm in pain or when something else comes at me? I pretty much suck at the whole word thing."

"I don't know what I'm going to do, Arden," Liam said honestly, looking down at their joined hands. "But I guess I have time. I just wanted you to know why my head's been out of it, and why I've been off. But, considering that I've been off the entire time you've known me, maybe you didn't realize that."

Arden frowned and rolled over to her side a bit. Liam reached out as if to help her, then stopped.

"You need me to call someone?"

Hell, he didn't know what to do. She was hurting, that much was clear, and he didn't know how to help her.

"I'm fine. Well, as fine as I can be. I was just getting more comfortable. Or trying to. I'm not in excruciating pain or anything. Promise. I'll let you know if I need help. But back to our discussion, I figured something was wrong. Plus, you told me that something was going on. It's fine that you're figuring things out. As you can tell, I have a few things to figure out, too."

"So, how about I stop worrying about my problems and just try to help you? Because I feel like a selfish bastard for talking to you about my issues when you're sitting here in a hospital bed with an IV attached to your arm."

"No, I'm glad you told me. I'm happy that you trusted me enough for that." He watched as her throat worked when she swallowed. "But I don't know what to say other than, I'm sorry. And I'm here for you. And I'm glad that you talked to your dad. Are you going to talk to your mom?"

Liam didn't say anything for a moment, just ran his thumb over her hand and took in the softness of her skin as he touched her. "I will. I'm not...I'm not angry about the idea of what happened. Does that make sense?"

"It does."

"I'm not upset about how it happened, at least the things in the past. I'm just angry about the lying."

"And that's not all of it, is it?"

She asked the question softly, but he snorted. "No, it's not all of it. And I know it's stupid. I know that I am my siblings' actual brother. I know that I'm a Montgomery. I have the last name, after all. That's always been my name. And I know that people are adopted and marry into families all the time these days and they are always family. It's just...it's like I lost a part of myself. And I know I should just get over it, but I need time. I just don't know what to do in the meantime."

"Well, you're still hanging out with your brothers and sister. And you talked with your dad. Maybe once you talk to your mom, it'll make sense?"

"I'm afraid of what I might say when I talk to her. Because I don't want to hurt her. I love my mom. I can just be angry at the same time. You know?"

"I know. I hate that you're in pain at all."

"I would say ditto, but that would be kind of redundant. Let's stop talking about me so we can talk about you."

"Let's not. I'm sitting here with yellow skin, sweat probably all over me, and I feel like crap. Let's pretend that we're sitting on a beach somewhere drinking mojitos and enjoying the nice air on our skin."

Liam looked at her then and felt something inside him tug. He hadn't wanted to feel that. Hadn't wanted anything like that.

Distraction.

But, hell, she hadn't been only a distraction in far longer than he cared to admit.

He couldn't help that tug. She was just so damn strong, so...Arden no matter what happened to her. So, he reached out and cupped her face. "We can do that. Just imagine the music playing, and the waves hitting the beach, lulling us to sleep as we nap under an umbrella. Because I really don't need a sunburn."

That made her laugh, and he laughed with her, and then they talked about nothing. Because all the important things had been said, at least the important stuff for right then.

Once Arden finally fell asleep, Liam extracted his hand and tried to focus.

It was hard to. Because there was so much going on. And even though parts of him wanted to be selfish about it, he couldn't.

Because Arden was more important than any weirdness he might be feeling.

And that fact stunned him more than he thought possible.

There was a sound outside the door in the hallway, and Liam turned to see Cross standing in the doorway, frowning. The other man tipped his chin, and Liam stood up, taking one last look at Arden before he walked out to follow Arden's brother.

He had seen the other Brady siblings throughout the day, but they had been in and out, dealing with their own shit and, apparently, trusting Liam enough to take care of Arden. He was happy that they did that, but he had a feeling they were only giving him the reprieve for a moment. They loved their sister to the ends of the Earth, just like he loved Bristol and the rest of his siblings. He knew that they weren't going to give him the time alone for long. And he didn't mind that. Not when Arden needed her brothers, too.

"She asleep?" Cross asked, taking one of the seats in the hallway.

Liam took the chair next to him and nodded. He stretched out his legs, wincing a bit since his back wasn't really enjoying all the sitting in those chairs for so long.

"Yeah, she's tired, but she's going to be okay."

"No, she's not," Cross said. "Let's go for a walk." And then he got up quickly, and Liam followed him.

Okay, then.

"What do you mean she's not going to be okay?"

"Oh, these symptoms will go away. They'll find a new drug to help, and she will be back to her normal Arden self soon. Sometimes, she'll be a little tired, but most of the time, she'll be fine. For the most part. She won't look sick because that's how it works. It's an invisible illness for a reason. But she is sick, Liam. I don't know if you get that."

Liam frowned and crossed his arms over his chest. "Excuse me?"

"No, wait, you don't get to be angry. She's mine to protect. Our parents aren't here, but they'll be here in a minute if we need them. They just know that my brothers and I can take care of our baby sister. And they know that no matter how many times they drop everything to come here, it won't be the last time. And every time that Arden sees them do that, it breaks her a little bit. So, we try to give her space, even though she doesn't think we do. But Arden is sick. And it's not going away. There's no cure for lupus."

"I know that."

"I don't know that you do. Because other than days like today? She can go out and run and enjoy life. She can hike mountains, albeit a little slower than she'd probably like. Though mostly because she doesn't really enjoy running or hiking."

Cross laughed, but it didn't reach his eyes. "She can eat what she wants and have a blast for the most part. And then it starts. A little twinge here, a little ache there. And then she's not okay anymore. But people keep telling her that she doesn't look sick."

"She sure as fuck looks sick now," Liam growled, getting pissed off.

"Yeah, because this is the outward signs of it. Because she's in the middle of a bad flare and basically has been since we took her out into the sun that day." Cross ran his hand through his hair and cursed under his breath. "Am I saying that if we hadn't taken her out in the sun all day, even with a hat and all that sunscreen, that this wouldn't have happened? I don't know. Am I going to blame myself until the end of time? Fuck, yeah, I am. Because that's my baby sister in there, and there's nothing I can do for her. Do you get that? There's nothing I can do to make this go away. I can only try and make it better."

"I'm getting that," Liam said softly. "Because I had the same thoughts."

"Okay, then. So, don't be here if you're going to leave her."

The two of them faced each other in a hallway where there weren't a lot of others, and Liam just stared. "You're telling me to leave your sister?" He blinked. "Are you fucking kidding me? You're saying to leave her?" He knew he was almost shouting and repeating himself, but…seriously?

"Yeah. If you don't think this can last, I am. You need to go. Because I'm not going to watch her break again because someone she cares about leaves her when the going gets tough."

"Who the fuck are you to say that?"

"I'm her big brother. And, yeah, I'm an overprotective asshole. We all are. We've always been. She's our baby sister. When she was younger? She didn't have this. She was energetic and happy and spent as much time outdoors as she could. She thought she was going to do so much, but she didn't get to do any of that. I mean, I think she's done a lot. I think she's done amazing things in her life, but somewhere in the back of her mind, I can see that she thinks that she hasn't done enough. And it's because of the lupus. Anybody with an invisible autoimmune disease will likely feel that. I've been to the message boards, I've been to actual meetings of family members who have their loved ones dying in front of them. And there's nothing we can do. But I have watched my little sister lose too much already."

Liam froze at the word *dying*, swallowing hard. "She's not going to die," he growled out.

Cross shook his head and then ran his hand over his face. "No, this isn't going to kill her. I know that. Because we're not going to let it. I just sometimes think about the worst thing that could happen and then I can't stop thinking about it. It's my fault, and I'm never, ever going to let Arden see that. Okay?"

"I get you. It's my job to think of the worst, too."

"As a writer. Yeah, I can see that. But this isn't a book. This is her life. Your life. And after a while, sometimes, people don't stay. They move on with their lives. Even her ex moved on. He couldn't deal with the fact that, sometimes, she couldn't just leave and go have fun. Sometimes, she just didn't feel good enough or staying at home sounded more fun. Sometimes, she had to deal with stupid shit like her body trying to kill her. So I'm not going to let you hurt her. Okay? If you don't want to be here for the long haul, then go. If this is too much, I get it. Just go."

"Don't push me away," Liam growled, his voice dangerous. "Did you do that for the others? Did you have them stand here and listen to you try to protect your baby sister and end up hurting her more for it?" Cross flinched and shook his head. "No, they did that all on their own. They left. I didn't even have to warn them. You? I don't know how stubborn you are, but my sister is sick, and I don't want her to have to deal with anything else that might hurt her. Even you."

"I won't hurt her. I don't want to hurt her."

"Yeah, those two sentences don't mean the same thing. But I can see something in you, so don't fucking hurt her. Or I'll hurt you. You get me?"

Liam gave him a tight nod. "I get you. And I won't tell her that we had this conversation. Because I have a feeling that would hurt her, too."

"Thanks for that. I don't know what to do. She's my baby sister. And she has so much more light in her than any of us. And it pisses me the fuck off that all I can do is watch her when she has bad days."

"I'm beginning to realize how hard it is to be on the sidelines. Though it's harder for Arden."

"It'll always be harder for her. But I'll be there. And I really hope you will be, too. Because I don't want to hurt you, Liam. I kind of like you." He paused. "Moderately."

"I don't know where we are. She and I just started this relationship. But if I hurt her? I have a feeling I'm going to let you hurt me."

"And that is the most honest thing you could've said."

They stood looking at each other for a few more minutes, and then they walked away from one another, Cross pulling out his phone, most likely to call one of the other Bradys. Liam went back to Arden's room. She was awake, looking a little confused.

"Did I hear Cross's voice?" she asked, stretching. She looked better, a little less yellow, and that was good. Oh, she scared the fuck out of him.

"Yeah, he's out in the hallway. I think maybe talking to Prior?"

"Ah, I knew they gave me too much time alone. Brothers." She rolled her eyes and smiled.

"Yeah. Brothers." He took a seat next to her and stretched out, ignoring the twinge in his lower back. He'd just have to get used to sitting in these chairs. And that was an odd thought.

"So, tell me about Nash and Penny." She grinned as she said it, and he saw the light in her eyes, the one that was so bright that he hated when the pain dulled it.

"What do you want to know?"

"You ask that as if you're going to tell me anything. But, is he going to save her?"

"I hope so," he whispered, looking down at her hand as he slid his into hers.

"Good. Because love needs to win." He gave her hand a squeeze.

"Yeah. Yeah, it does."

CHAPTER 16

*a*rden had been home for three weeks now and felt like she was back to normal. Or at least, whatever normal was for her. Yes, she still had lupus that wasn't going away. But her body felt like it hadn't been kicked in a while, so that was something.

She had energy, her rash had gone away, and if she ignored the slight bruising in the crook of her elbow and hand from where she'd been stuck by the needles, she felt like nothing bad had happened.

Oh, she knew it had. She knew her liver had taken a beating, and the rest of her body had gone along with it, but she was fine.

She was home, and she was okay.

And, later that night, Liam was going to come over, and they were going to watch a movie. They weren't going out for a fancy date where'd she'd put on makeup and get dressed and be all energetic—but she could if she wanted to. Tonight, however, was just about them and watching a movie. She'd done the date three nights ago where she had put on heels and makeup. That had been fun. Coming home where he had made sweet love to her had been fun, too.

She still couldn't believe that she and Liam had been dating for as long as they had. Considering that she kept pulling part of herself away from him because she was afraid of getting hurt, she was *really* surprised.

But she wasn't going to worry about that just then. They were dating. She was healthy for the time being. So, she was going to live in the moment. And to do that, she had to focus on work.

And the project she currently had was doing history searches for Liam's current book. Apparently, he needed help with a few outlying issues for the second half of the book that he was working on.

He had told her ahead of time that he was asking his editor for a double-check and more background, stuff that Liam had done on his own, but he wanted to see if there was anything else.

And so, they had gone through the correct channels instead of him just asking her directly. She would've done it for him regardless, but she kind of liked the fact that even though she didn't technically work for him, it was nice that he kept their work and private lives separate. That meant she could get paid for what she was doing, and pay that hefty bill that was on the way from the hospital.

No, she wasn't going to think about that. Not right now. She was just fine thinking about Nash and Penny and where the two of them were headed. Of course, that made Arden think about where she and Liam were headed, but she wasn't going to think about that either.

Not today. Today, she was going to delve into the worlds of Nash and Penny. And then maybe she would go out to lunch and treat herself to something nice. And then she'd have a date with Liam.

Sounded like the perfect scenario to her.

So, she threw herself into her book—or rather, Liam's book. However, when she was working on it, she did kind of feel like it was hers. A bit.

Today wasn't about anything except the analytical parts. Making sure that things made sense and were historically accurate. Because while it was historical fiction and Liam would make some things up like he always did, other things had to be correct, or readers would blow a gasket. She'd probably blow a gasket too since she needed things to make sense. And if Arden were honest, she really wanted to know what was going to happen with Nash. She wanted to know what he would choose.

Would he die? Would Penny? Or would they live happily ever after?

Arden didn't think the latter was quite there yet. Considering that Liam didn't write romance, it wouldn't really make sense for them to go off into the sunset. Not that there were many sunsets at the ends of the books she read. Well, now she was just going to have to find a romance where they actually did ride off into the sunset. That would be kind of interesting.

And, that was enough of that. Time to work.

She was lying on her oversized chair in her living room as she worked, using her internet for research rather than any of her texts just because she was able to for the day. And as long as she was comfortable, she would hopefully fend off another flare.

That made her snort. Yeah, like you could actually do that with lupus. But a girl could dream.

Jasper was sharing the ottoman at the end of the chair with her feet, meaning she was using her Husky as a footrest rather than the actual furniture itself, but she didn't mind.

Sure, she should probably keep her dog off the furniture, but that was never going to happen. Jasper slept with her in bed—much to Liam's dismay whenever the dog joined them after some cuddling.

That made Arden snort.

Yeah, a wet dog nose in places that should be far away from that wasn't the greatest way to end an evening.

She grinned, thinking about the fact that Jasper and Liam were getting to know each other. The two men in her immediate life. As long as they got along, that meant something.

And then they would just have to make sure the other four men in her life, her big, bad brothers and her dad, who was number five, all got along.

No, this wasn't complicated at all.

Once again, she pushed those thoughts out of her mind and went back to work, throwing herself into wars and different settings so she could make sure that the next L.M. Berry book was the best one yet.

The fact that she would leave her little touches on one of her favorite series of all time? It meant everything. The fact that it happened to be Liam's book? That meant even more. Even if it was a little weird.

By the time she finished her work for the day, knowing she had another compendium that she could work on later that afternoon, it was lunchtime, and her stomach rumbled.

"Okay, help me up," she said to Jasper as she closed her computer. He got off the ottoman, shook himself awake, and then reached out with his paw to pat her leg.

"You're such a good boy," she said, rubbing his head.

She used her feet to kick the ottoman out, and Jasper

helped her, leaning his body into it. Then she got off the chair, grateful that her boy was there, not leaning into her, but there just in case she needed him.

He really was the best dog in existence. Even if he still liked to try and get into her baking.

That reminded her, she hadn't baked since her last hospital visit, and while the people at the community center and the senior center understood, she missed it. And she missed her people. So, she would make sure she got some baking done because it not only made her happy, she also knew it made others happy. Or at least gave them some light in their darkness. She was just setting her computer down when the doorbell rang. She frowned.

"Wonder who that could be," she asked her dog, who seemed on alert as he padded over to the door, looking over his shoulder at her as she came towards him.

"I'm on my way," she said, brushing the top of Jasper's head with her hand. Then she looked through the peephole and smiled.

"Bristol," she said, partly opening the door. "I didn't know you were coming over."

"Well, I finished practice, and I wanted coffee and maybe a sandwich or something. Since I was driving near here, I thought I'd stop by. And I know that, like Liam, you probably hate people just dropping by when you're at work, even if it's your house. So, you can tell me to go, and I will. But I thought I'd see what you were up to."

And see how Arden was feeling.

Bristol didn't say that, but she figured. The entire Montgomery clan knew what had happened to her by now, even if Arden didn't know them all yet.

But she had a feeling that if Liam let his family, they would all be over trying to make her feel better. Even his mother—a woman that he hadn't actually spoken to yet since the paternity reveal.

Arden knew that Liam was hurting, that all of them were, she just hoped that they figured it out soon. Because this type of break couldn't be healed after a while, at least not in the way they'd want it to.

"I was just thinking I needed lunch and might treat myself for a meal out. That sounds wonderful. Come on in. Let me put on some shoes."

"Do you need to take Jasper for a—?" Bristol cut herself off and then widened her eyes. "Liam said Jasper learned how to spell that word. So, do you need that?"

Bristol laughed. "I'm going to let him out in the back before we go. Maybe when we get back from lunch, we can take him for that."

Jasper's ears perked, and Arden knew that he knew what they were talking about. But it was fine, so she quickly let him out into the back yard to make sure he took care of his business and then kissed him on the top of the head before she got into Bristol's car. They headed to the same café that she had gone to with Liam on their maybe-first date.

That made Arden smile as they took a seat, and Bristol leaned forward. "What has you smiling?"

"I was just thinking about how I think my first date with your brother was here."

"You think?"

"Well, we met at the hospital as you know. But then we met again in the neighborhood when Liam found Jasper for me after Jasper ran off after a bunny."

"Liam told me that. I didn't realize that Jasper ran off like that."

"He's never done it before and hasn't done it since. I think that he was just having a weird day that day."

"Or it was fate," Bristol said, winking.

That made Arden's stomach clench, and she shook her head. "Or it was just a really tasty-smelling bunny."

"Okay, so I'm not having rabbit for lunch," Bristol said with a snort.

"Yeah, maybe something with only vegetables."

"Sounds like a plan. So, you guys came here that day, then?" Bristol asked as the waiter dropped off their drinks.

"Yes. And then we ended up going out after that."

Arden blushed and then quickly put in her order for a

Caesar salad minus the chicken, as well as a hefty dose of bread. She really wanted carbs.

Bristol ordered the same, and then, as the waitress left, her friend grinned mischievously.

"So, what has you blushing?"

"It's your brother. And I'm totally not talking about that."

Bristol snorted and put up her hands. "Yeah, I really shouldn't have asked that. Let's just pretend that everything is sweet and innocent. I'm totally not going to ask anything like that again."

"Yes, let's not. So, how was practice?"

"Same old, same old. I have an exhibition coming up, and then I might have to travel overseas because my agent is planning something that I'm not sure I'm comfortable with."

"If you're not comfortable with it, don't do it."

"No, it's not like that. It's more like I don't think I'm ready." She looked down at her fingers, playing with her napkin, and Arden studied the other woman.

Bristol was becoming a world-renowned cellist and not only performed classical music, she also did pop hits and other fun songs that made her a sensation for the online crowd. She loved what she did, that much was evident in Bristol's voice, but it was odd to think that such a talented woman could feel as if she weren't good enough.

"I think you're amazing, and I've only seen you play online. I haven't even seen you in real life."

Bristol ducked her head, looking shy. Which was weird because Arden wasn't sure she'd *ever* seen Bristol looking shy.

"Well, I guess we're going to have to change that. But I try not to think about who's actually in the audience when I play. I have never actually thought about my family being there. Because I might get all blushy."

"So, who do you not mind in the audience?"

"I don't like to think about anyone. But I guess, my agent. And Marcus. Mostly because he doesn't actually care what I sound like. Not that my family cares. You know what I mean."

"No, I actually don't," Arden said with a laugh.

"Marcus? He doesn't care that he's my friend. If I suck, I suck, and he tells me. It's refreshing. My parents? It's just that they always know that I'm going to be amazing, they've always been that type of parents. The ones that would never give me a participation trophy just because I did something but more of a, 'well, at least you tried,' even though they wouldn't say it like that. I'm not saying this right."

"They were supportive and wanted you to do whatever you wanted to make yourself happy?" Arden said, leaning back as their waiter dropped off their food. After saying "thanks," they both dove in.

"Yes, just like that. See? I kind of suck at words. That's why I'm usually silent."

Arden choked on her salad.

"Hey, my family is allowed to make fun of me and my attitude. You cannot." Bristol paused and then grinned. "Unless you become family. If you know what I mean."

Arden cleaned up the Diet Coke from her shirt and glowered. "I think you're being a little premature."

"Sure."

"So, you and Marcus?" Arden asked, turning the tables.

Bristol wiped the dressing from her chin as she laughed. They were not having a good afternoon when it came to actually eating or drinking correctly.

"Oh, not even in the slightest. I mean, he's hot. But we've never seen each other that way."

"Doth the lady protest too much?" Arden asked, grinning.

"No, I just think that Marcus likes a certain type of woman. And I like a certain type of man or woman. And I think of Marcus like a brother. Seriously. He's like one step away from being a Montgomery."

"Wow, so sure."

"Oh, I'm sure. And, yes, I get that you're just trying to make me not think about what the future may be between you and Liam, and that was mean. However, most people think that Marcus and I have slept together once or twice in our lives. Or that we're still dating. But we've never. I just like the fact that I can have a completely platonic relationship with a man or woman and not have to have sex with them. I mean, it helps that Marcus has seen me at my worst, completely throwing up and everything."

"Liam has seen me throwing up, too," Arden said, now picking at her salad.

Arden winced. "Yes, but that was when he was taking care of you. Did he see you throwing up after you went topless on the beach and got completely drunk and started making out with like four different people before throwing up on the floor? No? Didn't think so. Yes, college was fun. And I was stupid. But, so was Marcus."

Arden just snorted. "Okay, now I kind of get it. You guys are just...friends."

"You didn't need to pause before you said 'friends.' Yeah. I think that's really the only reason my brothers let Marcus hang out with me. I mean, you get the overprotective, though."

"Dear God, I think we could share overprotective stories for a lifetime."

"Well, that's the plan. Because you're stuck with me now. Just saying."

"Really?"

Bristol shrugged and played with the last of her bread. "I know that we've talked about the fact that you don't have many friends because of what happened in the past. And I'm sorry about that. But it is my goal to force you to be my friend for a long time. Not just because of you, though. You know my ex? The blogger? Or, you know, the influencer?"

Arden nodded. "You mentioned her."

"Well, when we broke up, we remained friends, but our mutual friends didn't know what to do. After a while, I realized that other than Marcus and some of my work associates, all of my friends were her friends, too. They sort of took sides, even though we hadn't. So, one thing led to another, and although I still have people that I hang out with, I kind of lost my close group. So, you're stuck with me for a while."

"Well, I kind of like being stuck with you. Though I haven't really gotten to know the rest of your family yet, you and Liam are kind of cool."

"I would hope that you think Liam is cool. You're sleeping with him, after all." Arden glared as she picked up the ice from the table, thankful that she had already drunk the last of her Coke before she dropped the glass.

"We are really not having a good day, are we?"

"Let's just say I'm glad that we're not actually out in full public instead of here with no one else. Because this is a little embarrassing."

Bristol laughed and then called for the check and a few extra napkins.

By the time she got home, and the two of them gave Jasper a walk, Arden was tired, but from having a good day, not from a flare. She was going to count that as a win. She changed into a new pair of jeans and a T-shirt, figuring she might change again later if she wanted to look cute for Liam. She wasn't exactly sure what the plan was for tonight other than a movie, but she really didn't feel like showing up with Caesar salad dressing and Diet Coke all over her clothes. Seriously, she and Bristol had issues.

She was on the floor, rolling around with Jasper even though she knew she'd probably regret it in the morning, when the doorbell rang again.

"I wonder who that could be," she said, laughing. She kissed the top of her dog's head and went to the door, opening it because she knew it was Liam. "Right on time." She looked down at the dog hair on her clothes and winced. "I was planning to change."

Liam just shook his head, grinned, and kissed her hard on the mouth.

Her toes curled, and her core tightened. Man, the guy could kiss, even just to say hello.

"Don't change on my account. We're going to end up with that dog sleeping, sprawled over our laps as we're watching the movie anyway. Might as well stay in what already has dog hair on it."

She pulled away so he could walk in, noticing the bags in his hands.

"Well, I don't think I own anything without dog hair anyway."

"I found that I've started to collect dog hair at my place, too," Liam said with a grin. "Your dog." As if Jasper knew they were talking about him, he lifted his head and flicked his tail.

Liam rolled his eyes, rubbed the dog's head and back, and then leaned in for another kiss with Arden.

"I got us Indian food, but the mildest kind ever for your stomach."

"I can do spicy most times," Arden said, taking the bag from him.

"I remember, but I didn't want to risk it tonight."

"So, what do we have?"

"Chicken korma and lamb rogan josh."

"That sounds amazing."

"And all the naan you could need. Okay, maybe not all the naan because I'm about to eat like three-quarters of it."

"Oh my God, my mouth is watering."

"Good." He kissed her again, his hand going to the back of her head, his fingers sifting through her hair as he pulled her closer. She could feel the hardness of him through his jeans pressing against her belly, and she groaned.

"It seems my mouth is watering for more than just food," he growled against her lips.

"We can reheat this, right?" she asked, her breath coming in pants.

"Hell, yeah." Somehow, the two of them ended up in the kitchen, the fridge open, and the food put away. Jasper stalked away, huffing out a breath. Arden didn't care.

Her mouth was on Liam's, and she just wanted more of him. His hand slid up the back of her shirt, undoing her bra as he ran his hands along her skin. Her breasts fell, but his hands were still on her, slowly moving their way down her back, over her butt, then back up the front to cup a breast.

She sucked in a breath, her head falling back.

"I love your hands."

"Fuck, Arden, I can't think when you're around. I love your breasts, your back, your body. I just can't stop touching you."

"Did I ask you to stop?" she asked, her voice a purr.

"I hope you don't, ever." And then he was kissing her again, his mouth roaming over her cheek, then her jaw and down her neck. He tugged off her shirt, and she lifted her arms so he could pull it over her head, her bra going with it.

When she tugged on the bottom of his shirt, he grinned against her mouth, and he let her lift his shirt over his head. And then her breasts were against his body, skin-to-skin as the coarse hair of his chest brushed against the softness of her puckered nipples.

The sensation sent a shockwave through her, and she pressed her thighs together, her clit pulsating at the friction.

"You're so fucking sexy," he growled, kissing her again, but when he went to kiss her between the breasts, she pushed him away. He shrugged in question.

"I need to do something first. Something I've been waiting to do."

And then she went to her knees, and he raised a brow.

"Fuck," he drawled out the word.

"Not your knees, baby. I don't want you to hurt them."

"You keep using that excuse, but you never let me play." She said the words as she undid his belt, and he swallowed hard.

"Fine, if you must." She saw the laughter in his eyes, even through the darkness that was seduction with a tinge of worry.

When he reached over her, she groaned. He pulled two kitchen towels out of the drawer so her knees wouldn't hurt.

It wasn't the best, it wasn't a pillow, but it was all that was within reach, and she wasn't letting him go. Slowly, she undid his zipper and then slid her hand under the waistband of his shorts.

"Jesus Christ," he growled. His hand was in her hair again, and she licked the skin below his belly and right above the waistband of his boxers.

"Salty," she grinned. "I want more." So she pulled him out and licked the very tip of his cock.

He was thick, pulsating in her hand, and he groaned, tightening his grip in her hair. She didn't care, she just wanted him. And the tugging felt good, so amazing, she could feel it in her core.

She explored him, licking the crown of his cock and then down the length of him, placing small kisses along his shaft even as he groaned.

When she licked back up from the bottom, cupping his balls in her hand, he groaned.

And then she looked up at him and swallowed the crown of him whole.

"God," he growled.

It seemed he couldn't say anything else, just kept grunting. And that's when Arden knew she had him.

She swallowed him a bit more, humming along his length as she used her hands to get the rest of him.

He groaned more, slowly rocking his hips so he slid in and out of her mouth, and she bobbed her head, wanting more of him. She tightened her grip ever so slightly, and he shook, his thighs pressed against her forearms. She swallowed more of him, wanting more. But before he could come down her throat, before he could finish, he pulled out. She whimpered.

But then his mouth was on hers, and his hands were on her butt, her legs around his waist.

Somehow, he'd undone her jeans and pulled them down to below her knees. Her ass was on the counter, both of them grasping for each other, gasping, breathing.

They tugged and pulled, and then he was inside her, one quick thrust. They both groaned. Arden let out a scream, wanting more. She arched into him, her breasts aching, needy. And then his lips were on her, sucking one nipple into his mouth, letting go with a bite before kissing the other. All the while, he thrust in and out of her, pulling her closer to the edge of the counter as he fucked her hard.

She couldn't breathe, couldn't think. He was inside her, surrounding her, and then his thumb was on her clit, and she came, clamping around his length as he thrust again, and again. But he didn't let go of himself or her clit. He pressed down again, and she came once more. Somehow, she came a second time. And then he filled her, shouting her name into her neck as he pumped once, then twice, and then stilled, holding her so close that she felt her nails dig into his back, and his body tremble along hers.

That had been hard, fast, and...everything.

And then she felt him fill her in a different way. She pulled back and met his gaze.

"Fuck," she gasped.

"Jesus Christ. How did I...how did I do that? I forgot a condom. What the fuck, Arden? I'm so sorry."

Horror filled his expression. He reached around for a paper towel, wet it in the sink right beside her, and then pulled out slowly to clean them both up.

He was shaking, a look of abject horror on his face.

So she kissed him. Then she put her hands on his cheeks, pulled him close, and kissed him again.

"It's okay," she whispered. "I forgot, too. It's not your fault."

"Hell yeah, it is. I'm supposed to be the one who remembers. I've been doing this for how long? I've never once forgotten a condom in my life. What the fuck, Arden? I am so sorry I did that to you. To us. I...I'm clean. I can go get results if you want. But I, uh, I went to get blood tests, you know, just to check everything after the news with my parents. And I guess...fuck, I'm so sorry."

"It's okay. I'm clean, too. We do a lot of tests for the lupus and things. And I'm on birth control. So, we should be fine."

"I'll get you the results. I promise."

"Same. It's okay, Liam." She petted his cheek and kissed him again. "You're taking care of me. It's okay."

He held her then, holding her close even in her

kitchen, both of them naked. And while part of her knew she'd have to bleach the place, she shoved that thought from her mind. She was only thinking of her—of Liam.

Because they'd been lost in the moment, and they had made a mistake, but it would be okay. Because she was on birth control, and there were other ways to make sure this didn't happen again.

They were safe.

And as he held her close and she knew that he just wanted to take care of her, it told her that she was one step closer to falling in love.

And that scared her more than what had been forgotten.

CHAPTER 17

*L*iam sat in his truck, telling himself that he was going to get out soon. He *had* to get out. It was just hard to do when he knew that he was being a chickenshit.

He knew he should have come to his mother before this. He knew it. He just hadn't made good decisions. He'd needed time to decompress, to think. Now, he felt like he had taken too long. No, a month wasn't a super long time in retrospect, but he knew he had hurt his mom.

She had been there for Liam his entire life, but the fact that everything he knew had all been based on a lie? That hurt him. He needed to figure out what to say. Because he'd taken his time, knew he didn't hate her. But he needed to figure out how they were going to be. How they were going to make this happen.

He'd just needed time. And he'd had it. Now, he needed to actually get out of the truck.

His fists tightened on the steering wheel, even if the engine was off, and he sighed.

He was here because of Arden. Because she had faced so much and kept going. He couldn't back away from his life because he was scared. She hadn't.

Hell, he had forgotten the fucking condom, and she had been the one to console him. Her. Yeah, they were both clean, yeah, she was on birth control, but what if something happened? What if, like with his mother, that small percentage occurred. He didn't know what pregnancy meant with lupus. He hadn't researched it because, frankly, it wasn't his place, and they weren't there yet.

What if he'd put her in danger because he forgot?

And because all of that was in his head, he knew he needed to at least fix *something*.

And that meant actually talking to his mom. And not being an asshole about it.

There was a soft tap on his window, and he froze before looking to the left.

"Your sister called and said you were coming," his dad said as Liam opened the door.

"Yeah, I told her and the others so they wouldn't think that I'm a complete jerk."

"No one thought you were a jerk, son."

His father flinched a little at that, and Liam figured that was the hard part now. Because Liam hadn't flinched. This was his dad.

No, he didn't really know what he was going to think about all of it later or what would come next, but the fact that his dad had flinched using the word *son*? That sucked.

It made him feel as if his heart were being ripped from his chest. It made the cavernous hole in his body pull on itself and make him feel like he was going to throw up.

"I still feel like an asshole sometimes," Liam said softly.

"I'm going to go drive around the block or something," his dad said.

"You should go to Ethan's. I think he was planning on calling you soon to make sure you were okay."

His dad snorted. "Ethan is as much of a meddler as Bristol, yet she's the one that gets the bad rap."

"Just like I'm the one that wrangles, and Aaron's the one that cleans up after us all."

"Well, you all do a pretty good job."

"You taught us."

"Don't hurt your mom," his dad whispered. "Please don't hurt your mom."

"I won't. It already hurts, though, doesn't it?"

"I won't leave if she's going to end up a mess," Timothy Montgomery said, his jaw tightening.

That same jaw that Liam had thought was his but wasn't. He needed to learn what to do. Learn how to figure it out. He had to. But it was going to take time. It was always going to take fucking time.

"Go to Ethan's. I'm sure Aaron will show up, and maybe Bristol, too. Let me and Mom talk."

"You're a good boy," his dad said, reaching around to give him a hug, and Liam got out of the car.

"I hope so. But, Dad?"

His dad swallowed hard and nodded. "Yeah?"

"I'm still not okay. And I don't know when I'm going to *be* okay. I hope you realize that."

"I do. But we're going to be here. No matter what." And without another word, his dad went and got into his SUV, hopefully driving over to Ethan's.

Liam sent his brother a text to give him a heads-up just in case, and Ethan sent back a thumbs-up emoji. Well, the other Montgomerys in his life were all set. Now, it was time for Liam to figure out what to do.

He didn't have to knock on the door. "Hey," his mom said, her hand over her heart. "I saw you parked out there. Didn't know when you were going to come in, so I sent your dad out."

Liam nodded, noticing the way her eyes had tightened with the word *dad*. Yeah, they were all having a problem with that. Maybe Liam just needed to get it out. What *it* was, though? He didn't know.

Because he did not want to be the bad guy in this. And he was afraid that if he yelled at his mom, if he did anything to make her cry even unintentionally, he would be the bad guy.

His mom took a step back, and he followed her, walking into the home that he had grown up in, the one that they had moved into when he was about two. Apparently, they had lived in a smaller apartment when he was born, one they had moved into soon after their wedding. Liam tried not to think about the fact that he didn't know if his father had lived there on his own first or if his mother had or if they'd gotten it together. He had never asked. Because they never talked about that time.

But they had moved here when he was a little kid, and all of his memories had been made here. When his brothers and sister were born, this is where they were raised.

It was where he'd had his scrapes kissed by his mom, all his booboos healed. Where he had snuck in his first girlfriend and then been yelled at and pulled by the ear into the living room while she was quietly driven home.

Apparently, he hadn't been too good at deceiving.

This was the house where he had sipped his first beer with Ethan, and their friend, Lincoln.

Even though they had been two years younger than

Liam, they had all been as thick as thieves, getting into things when they shouldn't, and pretty much being teenage assholes about everything.

They had watched over Bristol together here, made sure she was the sweet, innocent Montgomery.

Even though they all knew she wasn't.

They had all babied Aaron, probably to the point where he was the most spoiled of all of them, even though you couldn't really be too spoiled in their family.

Liam remembered Ethan helping him with his science and math homework when he was in high school, and then in college for that matter, even though Liam was the older brother.

He remembered sitting in this living room and telling his parents that he had gotten an offer to be a model, and his mom freaking out that it was some sexual predator instead of an actual agent.

The fact that he had been lucky that it *had* actually been an agent had been a blessing.

He'd been too stupid at the time, too young and sheltered and naive to actually realize that it had been a real concern.

He remembered sitting in his room, trying to drown out the endless hours of Bristol practicing her cello. Hours and hours of her becoming someone with decent talent, to finally becoming a brilliant artist.

He had spent hours in this house, watching Aaron

play with different types of mediums for his art over the years—charcoal and paints and paper. Pen and marker and photography. And then his brother had tried his hand at clay, buying an old turntable that he and Ethan and Liam had dragged into the garage.

They had been so scared that his parents would yell at them for moving things out of the way, but then their dad had come in and shown them how to fix the legs to make sure it was even. All the while, Bristol had been their lookout to make sure they didn't get caught.

It hadn't mattered that their dad knew what was going on all along.

And then when Aaron had found his love with glass-blowing, it had been Liam's money from his modeling gigs that had sent him to his first apprenticeship.

Aaron hadn't known that at the time, but he knew now. Not that Liam cared.

They all worked together. They were a family.

And it was really fucking weird to think that things could have been entirely different if this man named Steve had taken Liam in instead. If Liam had known at the time that he wasn't their true blood brother the way they were with each other.

"You have so many thoughts on your face, Liam."

He looked up at his mother's voice and frowned.

"What?"

She reached up, cupped his cheek, and then pulled her hand back as if stung.

He hadn't moved, but this was the first time they had been in the same room for almost a month. It was like she was a stranger but also wasn't. She was still the same mom he remembered, there was just a jagged edge to their relationship now that he wasn't sure they could fix. Then again, maybe the jagged edge was him.

"You're thinking so hard that I can see a thousand thoughts running over your face. Will you tell me what you're thinking?"

"Just about everything that's happened in this house. About how we all learned so much here, did so much. And yet no matter how far we ran, how far we've come or gone, we always come back here."

He shrugged and stuffed his hands into his pockets. "Weird to think, right?"

She nodded and played with her fingers as she looked down. "I come from a military family, you know that," she said.

Liam nodded. "Grandpa and Grandma, right? Both of them?"

"Yes, your grandpa was a lieutenant colonel in the military, and your grandmother was in the service for eight years until she didn't re-up and went on to be a GS12 in the civilian sector. So, she was still able to PCS with my father and me." She smiled at Liam's look. He wasn't military and didn't know most of the acronyms. "That means she was decently high on the pay grade and moved with us with orders of her own. So no matter where we went, though, we never actually had a family. No...I said that wrong. We had a family, we just didn't have roots. Didn't have a home. We moved from place to place, never being able to find a home that was truly ours. Yes, my parents have their own place down in Florida that they love, but it's something they made with just the two of them in mind. I never had a room there."

Liam nodded, understanding a little. "So, you made sure we each had our own rooms here."

"It wasn't easy. At first, the property we purchased here only had three bedrooms. Your father and I didn't have a lot of money, but we had finished school and were working on savings. Somehow, we ended up with four beautiful children and were able to build onto the house. And though you guys shared rooms occasionally when you were younger, we ended up with five bedrooms. Though I think Bristol will always say that hers was little more than a closet."

"Bristol always complained, but she never had to share with anyone. It's just because she was a girl." Liam smiled as he said it, but the expression was fleeting.

"We did everything for our kids, and for ourselves, too. I love our family. I love the fact that there are roots. That I have lived in this house for longer than I've lived anywhere in my life. Even if you add all those places together, it doesn't equal the time here. This is my home. This is where I want to be for the rest of my life. I want to one day see grandbabies here, and I want to grow old with your father and watch you guys all make your own families when the time's right."

She paused and smiled.

"What's that smile for?" Liam asked, cautious.

"Oh, just thinking about all of you finding the loves of your lives and the fact that Bristol has been telling me about a certain someone in yours."

"I'm really not going to talk about Arden right now, okay? Maybe later."

His mother looked as if he had hit her, and he wanted to curse himself.

"This just isn't the time for that. I'm going to tell you all about her. Later. I promise. For right now? We have other things to talk about. And I think you know that."

"I know."

"I'm not going to hide her from you." And then he cursed for real, and his mom didn't admonish him, so he figured that this was a turning point. "You hid so much from me. Even if it was a single name on one line of a piece of paper, you hid that from me."

"And I know that I said I did it for a reason, but that was never to hurt you. I didn't want to break what we had. Your father and I love each other. We loved each other then, too. We just couldn't figure out how to be together because we had such strong personalities. And when those clashed, we also had big tempers. But we figured it out. Only after something had already happened. And my parents were so adamant about the mistakes I was making, even if they tried to be supportive, that I wasn't sure I trusted my love. No, I trusted it. I just wasn't sure I trusted love at all at that point. I wasn't sure that your father wouldn't just leave me once I held you in my arms. I was so afraid that he wouldn't love you the way I did. I was so afraid I couldn't love you the way I should. I needed you to be in my arms before I figured out the next step. And I know that was probably the wrong thing to think, but I did it anyway."

"But you were honest." Liam sighed. "And I get that. You were scared. Afraid that Dad was going to leave you because you had another man's child. I get why you didn't get married right away. I even get the fact that you and Dad were separated and weren't actually a couple when you got with that guy, Steve."

"I hate the name Steve now, and I think it's because of all the secrets. But that's neither here nor there. I just…it was a little emotional at that point. I should have married your father right away, but I was a chicken."

"You have never been a chicken in your life, Mom."

"Thank you for that." She smiled then, and Liam reached out to grip her hand. "I love you, Liam."

"I love you, too, Mom. I just...I wish I knew more about that time. Will you tell me?"

"Do you want to know about him? Steve? I don't remember a lot. I didn't know a lot, to be honest. And I don't know what kind of person that makes me."

"No. Do not shame yourself. Do you hear me? Let me tell you, I can remember the faces and names of every woman I've ever slept with, but I don't know their hopes or fears or where they are now or what they're doing. I don't know every intricate detail about every single person. I didn't love them. Just like you didn't love that man. So, don't you dare shame yourself for that."

"I should probably get mad at you for mentioning the fact that you've slept with women and discarded them."

"I didn't say that," Liam growled.

"You're right. I'm sorry." She squeezed his hand.

"It's just, back then, I was ashamed. Shamed by myself. Your dad never made me feel that way. He loved you, Liam. From the first time he felt you kick against his hand, he loved you. He would have married me right then, but I had to wait. Because I was scared. And because I was scared, I messed things up."

"I love you," Liam repeated. "Yes, it's going to take me a while to really get over the lying. And there will always be a part of me that wonders what was separate and what makes me different. I can't help that. But I'm not going to be angry anymore. I don't think I can."

"I hope you're not angry. I don't want you to be. Because you're a Montgomery, son. You've always been. And you always will be."

"I,"—he let out a shuddering breath—"maybe. Maybe." And then he held her close. She snuggled into his chest and told him about their first apartment, and how he looked as a baby. And then she told him about his first steps and the fact that he had tried to be a big brother to Ethan, even though he'd only been two.

She told him how she'd felt when she held him for the first time, and how she'd felt with Ethan. And that, no matter what, it had felt the same. She had been a mom.

And Liam believed her.

Yeah, he was probably going to have that anger about the lying for a bit. And, yeah, everyone kept telling him that he was a Montgomery.

But, sometimes, it was hard to truly grasp that.

But he would be fine.

Because he had to be.

And even if he occasionally ran from them, he still had his family.

Because Montgomerys were forever.

He just had to remember that he was, in fact, a Montgomery. Maybe not by blood, but by the pure strength and grit that was their family.

And that's all that mattered.

CHAPTER 18

"Why am I nervous?" Arden asked herself as she set out her charcuterie board. Yes, cheese was going to save her. Not that she could eat a lot of it today because she couldn't eat much at all. Her stomach hurt, though not from a flareup, thank God. Because she was nervous. Anxious because she was going to take the next step with Liam.

Yes, the two of them had already slept together.

However, she was taking the next step into them being something...more.

She was going to have dinner with her brothers and Liam. At her house. With no other supervision. Just a lot of testosterone, and plenty of prayers.

Dear God. Maybe she needed more cheese. And wine. And tequila.

Strong arms wrapped around her waist, and she let out a sigh.

"Maybe we should cancel."

"You do realize I've met your brothers, right? All of them. One at a time. We've all been in the hospital together." Liam kissed her neck, slowly sliding her hair to the other side of her shoulders. She shuddered out a breath.

He placed another gentle kiss on her skin, and she licked her lips.

"None of that, mister. I cannot be all flushed and turned on when my brothers show up. There are rules, Liam Montgomery."

"Oh, I know there are."

"And I think you're just trying to fuck with my brothers. Right?"

"No," he said, laughing as he turned her in his arms. He pressed her back into the counter and then lowered his head, gently brushing his lips along hers. She sank into him, wanting more, and knowing she couldn't have it. At least not right then. Because the Brady brothers would be there at any moment, and then her life would get a little more complicated. As always.

Not that it wasn't already complicated. But having all four of her brothers and Liam in the same room where her family could interrogate him for long stretches of time over a meal? No, she wasn't really looking forward to that.

Even if a small part of her was because, hello, it meant that they were taking the next step in their relationship. What was only supposed to be a date, was only supposed to be her giving her number to a man whom she thought hadn't wanted to call her at all, was now turning into something more.

They were trying to take things slow, but ever since her jaundiced hospital visit, it felt like everything was going a little faster, a bit out of her control.

Maybe that was what she needed, though. Perhaps she needed to throw caution to the wind.

"What is going on in that head of yours?" Liam asked, tapping his finger between her brows.

She scowled at him and slid her fingers through his belt loops at his back.

She loved that they casually touched so often. As if it were their right and they could do it whenever they pleased. It made her feel like this was something more.

And maybe it was.

And that was good.

"You're still thinking."

"I'm just thinking about the fact that I really don't want to have to clean up body parts later."

"That's not what you were thinking. But maybe I'll let

you get away with that. We're not going to murder each other. I can handle your brothers."

"You say that now, but they've been warned about what's coming. They're going to start slow, pestering you until you're this sad little gazelle surrounded by lions. And then, suddenly, you're in pieces and bloody, and there's nothing left of you."

"That's a wonderful image right before dinner," Liam said with a laugh. "And, I'm Liam Montgomery. There's no way I'm ever going to be a fucking gazelle."

"Oh, I don't know, they made my last boyfriend a gazelle."

"My hands are currently on your ass right now, pressing you into my cock. Let's not discuss your past boyfriends, shall we?" He growled out the words, but she saw the laughter in his eyes.

"Liam."

"Don't *Liam* me. We will not discuss him. He doesn't matter."

There was a finality to his tone that sort of worried her, but she had a feeling it wasn't jealousy. More indignancy at the way her ex had hurt her. After all, she knew that Liam knew why the relationship had ended.

Because she had been sick.

But Liam had stayed.

And so she was going to put that in the plus column.

The whole meeting with her brothers? That was in the neutral column for now.

"And you're going to tell me that you were pure like driven snow before you met me?" she asked, her brows raised. She hadn't actually meant to ask that. She didn't really want to know the answer. After all, Liam was probably the hottest man she'd ever met in her life. He wasn't a young kid, had been a model, and was now a bestselling author. She was pretty sure that he'd had his fair share of women.

"I'm not going to answer that question, other than to say that you're special. How's that?"

She looked in his eyes, her breath catching, and wondered what he saw there. Special? He hadn't said that before. It was new. It was…she wasn't sure.

Maybe she could get used to that.

But before she could ask him what he'd meant, or even figure out what she *wanted* him to mean, the doorbell rang. And then there was the sound of a key in the door. Suddenly, her brothers were inside the house.

She quickly untangled herself from Liam and stomped towards her family.

"What did I say about just walking in? Is this an emergency? No. You can't just use your key. What's the point of ringing the doorbell?"

Prior handed her a bouquet of sunflowers and kissed

her on the cheek. She blinked and set them down on the table beside her, wanting her hands free so she could hug her siblings. "It was to warn you that we were walking in."

"Yeah, a warning," Macon said, kissing her on the other cheek as he walked past her with two bottles of wine in his hands.

"You guys brought things?" she asked, a little behind.

Nate hugged her close, kissed the top of her head, and then walked past her with two loaves of French bread in his arms.

"We never come to your house emptyhanded," Cross said, kissing her on the forehead. "We always bring food or something for you."

His hands were filled with a covered cake dish of some sort, and she just shook her head.

"I know, and I love that you bring me groceries and things. But I told you not to bring anything tonight."

"Yes, and then they called me to make sure that I knew that they were bringing bread, wine, and dessert."

She turned and narrowed her eyes at Liam. "And you didn't tell me?"

"I tried to, but then we got distracted." He winked, a far too pleased grin on his face. Oh, she remembered that *distraction*.

She blushed and then risked a glance at all four of her brothers, who were now just laughing and shaking their heads. They didn't glare. They didn't tear Liam limb from limb. That was a good sign. Right? They were on the right track.

Before she could think too hard on that, though, Jasper came prancing in, getting love and belly rubs from every single male in the house.

"I swear your dog is getting bigger," Cross said, narrowing his eyes.

"He is not. Be kind."

"I'm not saying fat," Cross mumbled. "I'm just saying that I feel like he's gotten taller. Can they do that?"

"No," Arden growled out. "Stop teasing my boy."

"He's just a big dog," Prior said, on his knees as he cooed at her very large white Siberian Husky. Jasper was in love, leaning into Prior's hands. "Yes, you are. You're such a big, good dog. Yes, you are."

"I swear to God, you guys are insane," she said. "But Jasper is a good dog. Yes, he is."

That made everybody laugh, and Jasper continued to get pets and love, and even a dog treat or two before he made his way to his bed. "Okay, so, Italian for dinner?" Macon asked, peeking into the oven.

"Yes, I'm making regular lasagna, and zucchini lasagna."

Macon winced. "Really?"

"You've had it before. You liked it. I could do without all the gluten sometimes," she said, raising her chin. "Plus, I know you like it."

"Yeah, but that doesn't mean I have to eat it every time."

She shook her head, smiling. "Are you afraid you're going to lose your man card by liking zucchini?" she asked, laughing.

Liam wrapped his arm around her shoulder, bringing her to his chest.

"Not quite sure vegetables are what do that," Liam said, laughing with her.

"I'm not afraid of that. Hell, I was just being the annoying brother. You don't have to talk about my man card." Macon raised his brows, and the rest of the guys in the room laughed when she put her face in her hands, trying not to think they were funny.

"I really can't with any of you guys."

"You know you love us," Prior said, his hand on Jasper's head.

"Maybe. But I could do without the lot of you sometimes."

"No, I think we're going to stick around for a while, be a part of your life a little bit more. Maybe ask about intentions and all of that," Cross said, glaring at Liam. She froze but then saw the laughter in Cross's gaze. She felt the rumble of Liam's chuckle against her back.

"So, are the five of you just egging each other on?" she asked, pulling away from Liam. He put his arm around her waist and tugged her back to his chest.

"We're just messing with you," Liam said as he kissed the top of her head.

She didn't miss the fact that all four of her brothers followed the movement, but they didn't say anything. Apparently, Liam was in the good column. For now. She had a feeling if he messed up, they would probably want to kick his ass.

But, somehow, they'd all bonded over the overprotective crap of being a big brother, and now she was going to have to deal with it.

Great.

"Do you act like this with Bristol?" she asked, looking up at Liam.

"Of course. And Aaron." Liam looked up and spoke to Arden's brothers. "Aaron's the baby of the family. Bristol is too, but Aaron's just a little bit younger. So, Ethan and I like to make sure we get really overprotective with them. Very growly big brother."

"As is your right," Cross said, and Arden flipped him off.

"Hey, that's not very nice, little sister."

"Yeah, I'm hurt," Prior said, putting his hand on his chest over his heart.

"Oh, screw all of you."

"Don't know where you learned that type of language, young lady," Macon said, peeking into the oven again.

"From all of you. And Mom and Dad. And if you open

that oven one more time and let any of the heat out, Macon Brady, I will kick you."

Macon quickly shut the oven and put his hands behind his back.

"What is it with you and the kicking?" he asked.

"Well, I don't want to hurt my hands. I need them to work. I can probably deal with kicking. Especially if I put on some steel-toed boots." She tapped her chin and ducked when Macon went for her. But Liam tucked her against his side and glared at her brother.

"Hey, hands off," Liam said, but he wasn't too serious about it, at least from the tone of his voice.

"Maybe we should say that about you and our baby sister," Macon said. "Our precious baby sister."

"Yes, our precious, innocent baby sister," Nate said.

"We're twins, Nate. Really? You're like, what? A minute older than I am. And do you really want me to tell you about innocent?" she asked, raising her chin. She knew she blushed, but they'd have to deal with her stories if they were going to keep calling her that in front of Liam. Liam knew precisely how *not* innocent she was, after all.

"Okay, that's enough of that," Cross said, holding up his hands. "I really, really do not want to know."

"No, you really don't."

"So, you said 'sister?'" Prior asked Liam, grinning.

"I'm really not going to answer that question," Liam said, standing a little straighter.

Uh-oh.

"You guys, let's not, shall we?"

"What? He has our sister. I'm just saying." Macon ducked when Cross reached out and tried to slap the back of his head.

"I would say my sister is off-limits, but then she would kick my ass. And so would Arden. However, I'm really not sure any of you guys would suit her."

"Hey, what's wrong with my brothers?" Arden asked at the same time her brothers asked what was wrong with them.

Liam held up his hands and shook his head.

"Nothing. I just think she's in love with someone else. I'm not saying that your brothers aren't good enough for her or she's not good enough for them. All I'm saying is that I think she is meant for someone else. Don't rip my head off, okay?"

"I wonder if we're thinking about the same person," Arden said, rubbing her hands together.

"I am not going to say it. Because if I do, Bristol will know I said it somehow, and then I will get in trouble. I don't want to get into trouble." Liam kissed the tip of her nose, and she grinned.

Damn it, it was hard not to want this man more and more. But she had to protect herself.

"That's really the best way to go about little sisters. Just do your best not to get into trouble." Cross reached out and fist-bumped Liam, and Arden just rolled her eyes.

"I really just can't with you guys."

"Eh, you'll get over it," Prior said, grinning. "Now, really, when's dinner?"

"Well, the salad and the cheese are ready, so we can start on that. Dinner is just warming in the oven. It's whenever you guys want to crack open that wine or some beer, or just sit here and try to talk about Bristol and me as if we don't actually have choices of our own."

"Oh, good, we've angered her," Nate said, grinning.

"I'm not angry. When I'm angry, you'll know."

Liam squeezed her waist.

"Yeah, I have a feeling we would know."

By the time they ate, finished the wine and a bunch of water, Arden felt as if she'd taken a step she hadn't known she'd been ready to take.

She was happy.

Her brothers liked Liam, and Liam seemed to get along with them. Considering that was actually a great feat, something she hadn't been sure would ever happen in her lifetime, that was saying something.

But they all got along. It was a good dinner, and soon, she would have dinner with the Montgomerys.

She knew that more things were going on with Liam,

stuff that he hadn't talked to her about—like his conversation with his mom—but things were moving forward.

Liam kissed the back of her neck, and she sighed.

Happy.

She was happy.

This could work.

Somehow, throughout it all, she had found someone that she was happy with.

She kept saying that word in her head. *Happy.* She was so afraid that if she reached out and tried to grasp it with her hands, it would slip away like sand through her fingertips.

Because what if this was just the start, the peek of something before it fell.

And while she tried not to be negative about life—she couldn't afford to be—when the hits came, they kept coming. And she became a bad luck penny. Where one thing hit her after another, and she couldn't hold on. She couldn't survive.

So, she didn't know if she wanted to reach out and grasp this happiness full-on. She didn't know if she could.

She was afraid if she did, the disappointment when everything broke, when everything faded away would be too much.

And, in the end, she'd end up far more shattered than she ever thought possible.

CHAPTER 19

*T*here was something about sitting in the tattoo shop he'd been coming to for years that just made him smile. The fact that Montgomery Ink was owned by two of his favorite cousins? Yeah, that made him happy.

"I'm surprised you didn't go down to Colorado Springs," Austin said, rolling his shoulders back as they went over the sketch one last time before they transferred it to a stencil.

Liam turned and studied the other man. Austin's long beard had been groomed and trimmed at the ends. He'd let his hair grow a bit since Liam had last seen him, and had it tied at the base of his neck. Liam wondered if he would shave it again like he had before. There was never much middle ground when it came to Austin—or any of the Montgomerys for that matter.

Liam had gone down to Colorado Springs often over the past year to help one of his cousins get through her divorce. She'd pulled away from the family, and Liam had forced himself into her life again so she couldn't hide.

The irony of that situation didn't escape him. He couldn't hide from his family either. So, he pushed those thoughts from his mind and went back to Austin's question. "I thought of going down there, but since I brought my girl here, I figured we'd stop in Denver first. The next tattoo can be in Colorado Springs at Montgomery Ink Too." Since Liam had over a dozen pieces at this point, that probably wasn't a lie.

Austin was one of the Denver Montgomerys and Liam's cousin. He was a couple of years older than Liam and had been working at this tattoo shop for what felt like maybe a decade at this point. Liam didn't know for sure, it just felt like the building, and the people who'd become part of the extended Montgomery family had always been part of it. Austin and his sister Maya had gone in together on the shop. Now, they had a full staff, a piercing section, a whole area in the back where there were extra rooms for privacy, and a waiting list that Liam knew could be years long if they let it. The fact that real estate in downtown Denver didn't come easily just told Liam how successful the place was.

It was so fruitful, in fact, that two of their other cousins had opened up a satellite shop in Colorado Springs called Montgomery Ink Too. Shep and Adrienne ran that place and were starting to get so busy that everyone was thinking about maybe opening a third shop in one of the other cities.

Since none of the Boulder Montgomerys were tattoo artists, Liam didn't feel like it would be there. But who knew? Maybe someone would move up there. Perhaps one of the kids in a few years since some were getting older. Not that old, but still. There was a lot of talent in the Montgomery family, a lot of artists, and it made Liam happy. Made him think that their mark would be left and would be around long after they were dust in the wind.

"Your girl a virgin?" Austin asked, grinning at Arden. He winked as he said it, and Liam knew the other man was kidding, just letting off some steam since Arden had seemed oddly nervous. Could be the shop, but Liam figured it was because she was meeting more of his family.

Arden just rolled her eyes and looked over Liam's shoulder as they went over the sketch.

"You're very lucky that Liam warned me that you would joke like that," she said, grinning.

"Actually, I'm fortunate that my wife didn't hear me say that," Austin said, chuckling. "She'd hit me and threaten my beard—something she loves by the way—but

Liam warned me you might be nervous, so I figured inappropriate jokes were the way to go. But, anyway, you got any tattoos?"

Liam flipped Austin off. There really wasn't another response to that statement.

Arden just smiled before nodding. "Nervous? He's the one getting the tattoo. Anyway, I have a couple, but I haven't gotten one in a few years. Mostly because, sometimes, my skin doesn't like it." At Austin's questioning gaze, she clarified. "I have lupus."

Liam rubbed her thigh, hating the fact that she was ever in pain, but she'd said that she was fine, and he was going to believe her. Even if he watched her like a hawk.

Austin nodded. "I get that. My wife had issues with her first tattoo with me, as well. And we have a few clients with autoimmune issues, as well as some with scars, mastectomies, and other sensitive areas where the experience is different. If you ever decide to get another one, we're the place to do it. Liam can vouch for us, but we'll do our best to keep you as pain-free as possible when you're with us."

Liam squeezed her hand, and she smiled at his cousin. "Thank you," she said, grinning. "I have a feeling I'd be in good hands."

Austin shrugged. "We're the best."

Humble, Austin was not, at least not in front of family where they could just be themselves.

"I guess since Liam drove us over an hour to get here, you must be well worth the drive. Traffic and all that."

Austin met Liam's gaze. "Oh, we are. Maya's going to be pissed that you scheduled with me and not her, though."

Liam rolled his eyes and handed over the sketch. "Maya had my arm last time. It's your turn this time. We're just adding the fleur-de-lis, right?"

Liam nodded. "Yep. You're going to have to start working on your other sleeve soon," Austin added.

"And most of my back. And my legs. Eventually, I'll be fully covered like you."

"I still have some open skin. I mean, I have a few more years left in me when it comes to tattoos, right?"

"Exactly," Liam agreed.

"Let me get this stenciled, and then we'll figure out exactly where we want to put it, even though we've already done enough placement. But you know me, measure eighteen times and ink once."

"Only eighteen?" Arden asked, her teeth worrying her lip.

Liam reached out and tugged her to his side.

"You okay there? Afraid of needles?"

"If I was afraid of needles, I think I'd be even more stressed out than I already am, considering all the needles I've had to deal with in my life."

Austin gave him a questioning look but didn't ask

more before he went back to the office. That left Liam and Arden alone. He wrapped his arms around her waist and tugged her onto his lap.

"Liam," she whispered with a laugh.

"What? It's not like you're going to sit on my lap for the whole tattoo. I mean, you could. I'm sure Austin would let that happen."

"Yeah, don't think so, man," a big, bald guy said from his station on the other side of the room. He had a broad chest, and Liam swore his arms could break anything in their path. He had a pretty woman with blond hair and dark red lips next to him, his wife from what Liam remembered. Liam just nodded. "He may be your cousin, but I'm pretty sure lap-sitting during a tattoo is a line," he said with a laugh.

"Yeah, I'm pretty sure, too," Liam said, nodding at the couple before turning back to Arden.

"I like it in here, though. And you're right. I would like to come back here if and when I'm ready for my next tattoo."

Liam nodded, and the idea of the Montgomery iris somewhere on her body warmed him.

What? Where the hell had that come from?

They weren't getting married. They hadn't even talked about it. In fact, they'd been very good about *not* talking about the future. They were just trying to live in the moment, something that neither of them had been able to do recently between his family life and her health.

So, they were just trying to *be*.

Picturing her with the Montgomery iris anywhere on her body wasn't something he could do. Because they weren't there yet. They weren't ready for marriage or babies.

He swallowed hard.

Babies? Hell, he wasn't sure he was ready to be a father—or if he ever would be.

Kids had never been on his radar, something that maybe should have worried him.

Hell, he really needed to stop thinking about all of that, stop getting so serious.

Arden wasn't his distraction anymore. They were getting serious, but they were a long ways from family crest tattoos and the idea of children.

At least, that's what he told himself.

"So, the fleur-de-lis is from your book, right?"

Liam nodded and looked down at his arm.

"I add symbols from my books if they hit the list." His earlier books hadn't hit the *New York Times* list until his third installment, and then a sale had pushed the others on at some point.

He shrugged, knowing his face was a little red.

"I know it sounds weird, but I wanted something to remember this by. I actually have a friend who has the symbols on their wall too, just hidden. Or at least the symbols from their books. I figured I would use things from my books in a little more permanent way. Mostly because ink runs in our veins. It's a family thing."

"Yeah, us Montgomerys are a little weird," Austin said as he came back.

"You ready to do some stenciling?"

"Always."

"Oh, this is going to be fun," Arden said, sliding off Liam's lap and onto the stool that Austin had pulled up for her.

"My brothers never let me sit and watch them get tattooed. Mostly because they think that I'll get squeamish or something." She rolled her eyes, and Liam leaned over and gave her a smacking kiss on the mouth.

"It's like they don't know you," he said, grinning.

"I know, right?"

"Seriously, the two of you are fricking adorable. Maya's going to be sad that she missed this." Austin went to work, grinning.

"Really?" Liam asked. "You're going to get that way on me?"

Liam bringing Arden to get his tattoo was like bringing her home to meet his family. He knew he probably should have done the family dinner thing first, but since things were a little iffy at home, he had done this instead. The rest of the Montgomerys didn't know about the family secret, but he figured he might actually let them know eventually. He just wasn't sure if it was his secret to tell.

Yeah, it was his birthright. But it was more about his parents. He didn't want to hurt them.

And the fact that he thought that? Thought of Timothy as his parent? Meant he was finally finding a place where he could settle.

And that meant something.

"What? The two of you *are* cute. Just saying. Once you go ink…" Austin trailed off, and Liam just snorted.

"Hey, so, how's the family?" Liam asked, wanting to get off that track since he and Arden probably needed to have another label conversation at some point. Or at least *a* conversation.

Austin smiled in a way that said he had secrets and was one damn happy man. He'd drifted for so long that it was nice to see him settled and happy. Liam wasn't as close to Austin as he was with some of the other members of his family, but he'd grown up just a few years behind Austin. And considering that some of the other cousins in the family were far younger, the age gap wasn't too bad.

"Wife's good, she's across the street at her shop. They're talking about opening another one in Centennial, but I don't know if we're ready for that."

"Yeah, you already have the two tattoo shops. Things add up."

"Oh, I don't really have to do much with the one down in Colorado Springs. And I don't think Sierra would have to do a lot with the other boutique once it was open, but we've got a family. And since we're still waiting to hear about the adoption process, we're sort of in limbo."

"You're adopting?" Arden asked and then winced. "You don't have to talk about it with me if you don't want to." Liam rubbed her arm, and they held hands.

"I wouldn't have said anything in front of you if it was an issue for me," Austin said casually as he worked with the stencil. "But it's a long process, and since we own our own businesses, and I don't look like typical *father material* sometimes, it gets a little confusing."

"And you already have two kids, right?" Arden asked. "Does that matter?"

"Everything matters to the system. But we're working on foster to adopt first. And we're both ready to take in older kids. Not just babies. So, hopefully, that's a mark for us."

"Considering your kid's like twenty now, that should be a point in your favor, right?"

"I'm about to put a needle into your skin. So, fuck off. Leif isn't even old enough to drive yet." Austin paused. "He's close. But I don't want to talk about that."

Liam grinned and looked over at Arden. "He has an almost-ready-to-drive child, and I think one in elementary school. Or preschool. Right?"

"Yep, age gap's a bit. But Leif is amazing with Colin. It's so weird sometimes to think that I'm a dad, you know? Never thought it would happen. But here I am. In fact, most of the Montgomerys are parents now."

"Yeah, you all decided to pop out babies in the same year or something."

"Dear God, the amount of pregnancy hormones going on during that year." Austin gave a full body shudder. "You're just lucky that you were on deadline and holed up in your little writing cave during that time. That's all I'm saying."

"Yeah, that was a lot of babies."

"None of my brothers have had kids yet, so I'm a little worried what's going to happen when they become dads. They're overprotective enough."

"How many brothers do you have?" Austin asked as he started working.

The buzz slid into Liam's ears, and he relaxed. He liked the feeling of the endorphin rush, the sound, and even the needle in his skin. It wasn't like getting his blood drawn or even getting a shot. It was just a little pressure, a slight sting, over and over. The shading was his favorite part, maybe that made him a little bit of a masochist, but anybody who liked getting tattoos? They had that in them.

"I have four," she said, and Austin smiled, laughter in his eyes. He went back to work, and Liam relaxed under the somewhat pleasurable pain.

"Talk to me when you have seven siblings."

"Seven?"

"Yep. Seven."

"Bristol wasn't kidding when she said that there were a lot of Montgomerys."

"Yeah. There are five up in Fort Collins. I think four in Boulder. And four down in Colorado Springs. Us Denver ones, we're the larger group."

"And then when they all start having children?" Liam shuddered. "It's like bunnies. So many bunnies."

"Well, it sounds like you guys are happy," Arden said, looking over Liam's shoulder as Austin worked.

"Yep. We found our bliss."

"Where is Maya, by the way?" Liam asked, relaxing.

"She wanted to be here for this, but both of her men and her kids are down with colds. That means she's running hazard over the house. She not only didn't want to bring germs in here, but two man colds and two kid colds? I do not envy her."

"God, that sucks," Liam said.

"Two men?" Arden asked. She asked as if she were intrigued and not judging, and Liam was glad for that.

Not everyone in the world was understanding of Maya's relationship, but the family was happy, and that's all that mattered.

Liam looked over his shoulder and narrowed his eyes. "One is enough for you, missy."

"So you say," she said with a laugh. "My friend is in a ménage relationship, as well, so I just think it's cool that there's another one down here. Sorry."

"Don't be sorry. But remember, I don't share." And then he kissed her, and he heard Austin's laugh even as he kept working.

They talked for a bit more, but it didn't take long for Austin to get the small fleur-de-lis finished.

They went over aftercare instructions like usual, even if this was far from the first tattoo he'd gotten.

And then he said goodbye to his cousin and the rest of the crew, and left a note for Maya and her men, even with a little signature from Arden because she was part of him now. It was kind of nice.

They made the drive back up to Boulder, thankfully missing rush-hour traffic, both of them just talking about books and nothing in particular, just the way he wanted it.

As they held hands, he looked down at their linked fingers for just a moment before shifting his gaze back to the road. And then he wondered how this had happened.

How had he ended up with Arden?

He hadn't known that he wanted this. Hadn't known it could become anything at all.

But he was enjoying himself, and he was happy, and though things could change at any moment, and he knew damn well that they just might, he was going to live in the moment. And he was kind of excited to see what the next moment would bring.

They pulled into Arden's driveway and jumped out, Arden moving quickly because they had left Jasper alone for longer than they had planned.

Jasper walked around the living room, leash in his mouth, and Liam just rolled his eyes.

"Why don't I go take him for a walk and let you rest for a bit?"

Arden just narrowed her eyes. "I can go with you. I'm doing fine. Let me be."

"Okay," Liam said, hooking the leash on Jasper's collar.

The dog barked twice, and then they were off, going for a walk as if this were something they did every day. As if this was their life.

And Liam liked it.

He liked it a lot.

By the time they got home and started thinking about dinner, Liam wanted more.

He'd had Arden next to him all day, and had only stolen a few kisses, a few touches.

When he leaned down and took her lips with his, she moaned, and he knew he didn't want to wait until after dinner.

"Liam?"

"I just want to kiss you."

"From the feel of you beneath the zipper of your jeans, I have a feeling you want more than kissing," she said, biting his chin. "Are you sure you can with your tattoo?"

He snorted, kissing along her neck, loving the way she arched into him. He loved nibbling on her neck, adored the fact that it was such an erogenous zone for her. He knew she'd be wet just from his touches.

Because, damn it, he could practically smell her arousal, she was so pliant in his arms, so soft.

He wanted to go slow, but he wasn't sure he could. Not now. Maybe not even when it came to her in general. He wanted to give her roses and softness and delicateness. But there was no way he could. Not with her. He wanted to be wrapped around her, have her scent wrapped around him.

He wanted everything.

And it scared him.

So, he pushed it from his mind and just gave in.

"I got a tattoo on my arm, Arden. Not my dick."

"Really? It's like I wasn't sitting next to you when it happened or something." She pushed his chest, and then leaned forward again to kiss him. "But I don't know if I really want you to get your dick tattooed. It's really pretty as it is."

"My dick is pretty?" he asked, slowly undoing the buttons on her blouse. Since she was working on his belt, he just grinned. They undressed each other slowly, even as they talked. And, damn it, he couldn't wait to fuck her. Couldn't wait to sink inside her and maybe go slow—but probably not. Just hard. Hard and fast and all his.

That was his Arden. His.

"Yes, I think your dick is pretty. Especially when it's in my mouth."

"Look at you with the dirty talk."

"Hey, I read."

"So do I, but I don't think I'm reading the right books."

"I'll read them to you before bed if you want," she said, sinking to her knees as she slowly wrapped her lips around him.

He groaned, the feel of her warm mouth surrounding his cock so good that he almost blew his load right there. Instead, he slid his hands through her hair and rocked himself in and out of her mouth, one stroke, then two.

She hummed along his length, and the vibration went straight to his balls, right to the base of his spine.

And so he curled his toes, toeing off his shoes as he did so, and tried not to come right then. But it was so damn hard with the sight of Arden shirtless, her breasts bare and ready for his touch as she knelt, looking up at him with his cock slowly sliding in and out from between her plump lips.

"Jesus, I can't wait," he said, pulling out. His dick was wet, and she pouted at him, but then she grinned as he lowered to the floor, helping her undo her pants. Then she was naked and on her back, her hands on her breasts, plucking at her nipples as he licked and sucked at her pussy.

She had one leg over his shoulder, the other pressed down to the floor as she writhed under him. So, he put one arm over her waist, pinning her down, and used the other to spread her so he could get to her clit easier.

"Liam," she gasped. "Be careful of your arm."

"Don't worry, I'll be on top, less floor burn that way," he growled.

"But what about me?"

He hummed along her clit and then bit at it gently. And then he sucked, twisting his lips just right. She came, screaming his name.

"I'll be gentle," he groaned, and then he was between her legs, holding the base of his cock as he slowly slid into her, meeting her gaze inch by inch, stroke by stroke.

And when he hovered over her, slowly sliding in and out of her as she wrapped her legs around his waist, he leaned on his good arm and used the other to run his hand down her sides, hold her hips higher, and just be near her, touching her.

She was so tight, so his, and so fucking perfect.

He loved every inch of her, adored every scar, every bruise, every curve.

He loved her body. And he had a feeling if he let himself, he could admit that what he felt was love. But he didn't let that happen. Didn't think about that. Because what if he lost her? What if she decided that he was too much? What if this was just her distraction?

And as she came again, his thumb on her clit, he pushed those thoughts from his mind. This was their moment.

He couldn't think about anything else. He could only think about her and this moment.

Just this moment.

And then he came, growling her name, his lips on hers as he dove in for a deep kiss, slamming into her one more time.

Just this moment, he reminded himself. And this moment was worth everything.

CHAPTER 20

*A*rden should have known that everything had been going too smoothly for the past couple of weeks.

She had been immersed in her work, loving her job, adoring every single little detail, even the ones that made her eyes cross as she tried to cross-check the color of a side character's eyes over eighteen books.

But she loved it.

She had spent almost every evening with Liam, either at her house or his. And Jasper had been along for the ride every time, finding his own space in Liam's home.

It was as if they had taken this next step and were a couple in truth, looking towards the future. It was just so odd to think that it was happening at all, that they were making things happen without stressing about it. They were just being themselves, and it was working.

And Arden's family was actually giving her some space, all the while being there when she needed them.

They were getting along with Liam, and Liam even looked a little lighter than usual lately, as if he could finally breathe a bit after having talked with his mother.

And Arden's health was doing better. She had been feeling good, lately. Had even gone on a little jog with Liam, though not a long one. Okay, she had walked really quickly while he ran around the loop twice. She only did it once. And, yes, he had made the on your left joke from *Captain America*, and she had fallen just a little bit more in love with him after that.

It was the perfect cherry on top after a really good couple of weeks.

But she should have known it wouldn't stay like that.

Because how could it?

She quickly rinsed out her mouth, brushing her teeth, and then went back to cleaning the rest of the bathroom after her sickness. She had thrown up three times that day and hadn't been able to keep any food down.

That was new for her. Something that hadn't happened in a while.

Her whole body felt cramped, but mostly her lower half, and she was getting a little worried.

She hadn't felt like this...ever, now that she thought

about it. Were these new symptoms? Was she getting a flare to end all other flares?

She didn't know, but she was really tired of being sick.

She had plans to meet with Liam later, and while the two of them planned to go out to dinner and then over to Ethan's house for a movie, she wasn't sure she had it in her.

Her whole body just hurt.

She took a couple of steps towards Jasper, who was giving her a very worried look, and she gagged, throwing her hand over her mouth before running back to the toilet and heaving.

At this point, it was only dry heaves.

She had nothing left in her stomach except bile. And wasn't that pleasant?

She let her body do its thing, and then cleaned up the bathroom again, brushed her teeth once more, and got a washrag from her linen closet so she could put it under some cool water for her forehead.

God, she felt horrible.

It was almost as if this sickness just came and went with no idea what it was doing.

And then she froze, trying to do the math.

When had she had her period last?

She was highly irregular thanks to the lupus and her endometriosis. Those two things together were not fun.

And her other acquaintances at the hospital and in the

message boards with lupus tended to have endometriosis, as well.

So, she couldn't always rely on her period math to figure out if she was late or not. Because she was always late.

But now, she was really late.

She ran to the toilet again, dry heaved, and then sat on the floor, her head in her hands as she tried to figure out if she was indeed pregnant.

She and Liam hadn't talked about that. Yes, they had foregone condoms, but she was on birth control.

But what if it wasn't enough?

Because condoms weren't one hundred percent effective. And neither was birth control.

"Dear God."

So, instead of going to the grocery store and picking up a test, she called her doctor.

She might as well be entirely sure, and since she wasn't feeling great as it was, she might as well see them and ask if it was part of her endometriosis, or maybe her lupus. Or perhaps she had a brand-new thing that was going to knock her on her ass.

Why couldn't she be happy?

Why couldn't she have just one pain-free month in her life?

"And if you whine about it a little bit more, maybe it'll help," she whispered to herself.

"I just need to breathe," she said, letting out a breath. "Just breathe."

Her doctor was able to fit her in within the next hour because of a cancellation, so she quickly threw on some clothes, hugged her dog, and made her way to the hospital.

All of her doctors were in the same big hospital near her house. She was grateful for that. She didn't have to drive all over the city.

But it also meant that waiting times to get in to her specialists were ridiculous.

She was really grateful that she had been able to get in to her doctor for this.

Maybe that was a good thing. Perhaps it meant that it was just a typical day feeling like crap where she would feel fine later.

And if she kept telling herself that, maybe it would become true.

She texted Liam to let him know where she was going but just said that she had a doctor's appointment so she didn't alarm him.

He didn't text back right away, and she figured that he was stuck in his writing cave. After all, he had the last parts of the book going. He probably wouldn't have noticed if there was an actual fire in his home at this point.

But that was fine. Arden didn't really want to tell him

more about what she was doing. Because what if she was just freaking out for nothing? She probably was.

By the time Arden got to the room and talked to her doctor, she just nodded softly and went about asking questions and taking some tests.

It took over an hour, but she was just lying there on the bed, still waiting for a text from Liam yet knowing that she was fine. Everything would be fine.

"Okay, Miss Brady, we have news."

Arden sat up, her heart beating fast in her chest.

"Yes?"

"First, you're not pregnant," her OB/GYN said quickly, and Arden let out a relieved breath.

"Thank God. I mean, not that babies aren't great and everything, but we aren't ready, I'm not ready. And with everything else going on…"

"Yeah. We're going to come back to that in a moment. But I'm going to let you know that we're going to admit you. Not here, but on the other side of the hospital."

"Excuse me?" Arden asked, putting her hands over her stomach.

"I thought you said I wasn't pregnant. Is it just a bug?"

"No, it looks like you might have pancreatitis. You're going to be fine. But we're going to give you some IV antibiotics just in case, and do some more tests that I can't do here. Okay? But you definitely need some meds, and intravenous is the way to go, especially with your medical history and the amount of pain you're in. I'm not your doctor for your lupus, but I'm sure you know that pancreatitis is a symptom."

"I get it. My body's attacking my organs." She swallowed hard and quickly wiped the tears from her face. She hadn't even realized she was crying.

Pancreatitis? Another fucking organ? She had been doing so well for so long, and now it was hit after hit. Why couldn't she just catch a break?

Her doctor handed over a tissue and gave her a slight smile, one that reached the doctor's eyes but didn't feel pitying.

Arden loved her team, she really did. They listened to her and never told her that she had to lose weight in order to not feel pain. She was blessed with these people. And yet she wanted to punch something. She just wanted things to be okay.

But it wasn't okay. Her hands shook, and then another wave of pain hit her, and she pressed her lips together, trying not to throw up or feel like she just needed to cry and fall.

"Okay, let's talk for a minute, and then I'm getting you over there, okay? You're going to be okay, Arden. Your other doctors can talk to you about this, can go into every single little detail you want. I just know this must be a lot for you. Your lupus has been acting a little aggressively for the past couple of months, and that happens. But you can get out of this flare, and then you can be perfectly fine. You know that. You were fine for years. Stable. We just need to get you out of this cycle, and then you'll be okay."

Arden sniffed and wiped her face. "I know. It was my skin, and then my liver, and now, my pancreas?"

"It's all connected. You know this. And while I'm an OB/GYN, I can tell you that I have talked with your doctors, and they're going to give you a full treatment plan. They have high hopes."

"Don't lie to me," Arden said, wiping the rest of her tears away.

"They do have high hopes. Because you're strong. And while there is no cure for lupus, they're going to find a treatment plan that works for you so you're more comfortable and not always in so much pain or so symptomatic. Okay? Now, I have something else to talk to you about."

Arden sat there and listened and tried not to throw up again, she just tried to breathe.

Because as her doctor kept speaking, Arden watched one more part of her life, something she hadn't even known she wanted, slip through her fingers.

And she didn't want to listen anymore. She didn't want to know anything else.

Because her body hated her. And right then? She kind of hated herself.

She just wanted a happy ending. She just wanted to be happy.

She wanted to tell Liam that she loved him and that she was going to be there for him. She wanted to watch her brothers fall in love with their future mates, and she wanted nieces and nephews and a whole big family. She wanted to get to know Liam's family and watch as they tangled with their own relationships.

She wanted all of that. And she was so afraid that she wasn't going to get it.

So, so afraid.

They moved her over to a room a couple of hours after that—timing in hospitals always seeming to stretch on forever.

She was hooked up to more IVs but feeling a bit better. At least physically. Mentally? It was like one blow after another.

Cross showed up right away, holding her hand as she went through details about the pancreatitis. She didn't tell him the other part. No, that was something just for her. At least for now.

And maybe Liam.

She was just so tired. So exhausted, in fact, so used to this happening, that she had a go-bag for medical emergencies. Cross hadn't brought it with him, though. He'd said that Liam was on his way, and that made her feel a little better. Liam hadn't texted her back, but he'd apparently gotten her message. Then he had told the rest of her family what was going on.

Maybe he didn't know what to say in a text. After all, she wasn't really sure what to say either.

When Liam showed up, Cross left the room after hugging her hard and saying he would be back a little bit later, maybe with her other brothers.

She loved them, she really did.

"Hey, you," Liam said, dropping the bag.

"So, I broke my phone. I got pissed off at a scene and threw it. But I saw that I got a text from you, I just couldn't actually text you back. So I used Ethan's phone to call your brother since, for some reason, he has all of your numbers. I'm pretty sure he has every single number of every person he's ever met just for emergencies. He's like that. Anyway, I'm sorry I didn't call, but Ethan is helping me get a new phone, so I can hang out here with you while we figure this new thing out."

He kissed her on her forehead and then gripped her hand. "How are you?"

"I've been better," Arden said, smiling at him. "You sound like you've had a bad day."

He snorted. "Yeah, let's not talk about bad days. You're the one in the hospital. I've just got a character who's pissing me off. But that's every book. So, pancreatitis?"

"It's a very mild case. I just happened to get hit with it a little harder with the symptoms. It should be cleared up soon, and then I'll be back to normal. My rheumatologist and I are going to talk about some more treatments. That way, maybe I can stop getting hit with one thing after another. I don't think the drug I'm on is doing its job."

"I would think not. But we're going to figure it out. Don't worry, I'm here."

The way he said that, it was as if he actually were. That he was sure. She couldn't take it anymore. Tears spilled down her cheeks. She sat up, covering her face with her hands.

This hurt. It hurt so much. And it was so hard to think of a future when everything was breaking down.

"Talk to me. What's wrong, Arden? Are you scared? It's okay. I'm scared, too, but we're going to get through this together. I promise."

He cupped her face and wiped her tears away. She just leaned into his hold, needing to tell him the other news.

"It's not that. I mean, it is, but it's also something else."

She pulled away, and he reached behind her for a tissue, wiping her face.

"You can tell me. You can tell me anything. After all, I told you I was a secret baby, it's one of your favorite tropes in romance. You can tell me this, too."

She let out a watery laugh and shook her head. "You need to sit down."

"Okay," he said, his expression serious.

"You should know that I came here initially because I thought I might be pregnant," she said quickly. Liam's eyes widened.

"What? Are you?"

There was such hope in his voice, tinged with a little fear—exactly how she had felt. She shook her head, wiping away another tear.

"No. And we did an ultrasound while we were checking up on everything. It seems my endometriosis is getting worse. Probably because of all the drugs I'm on and the fact that my body's attacking every organ."

"You said you were having pain," he whispered. "So, what does that mean?"

She picked at a thread on her sheet, wishing she were healthy. How hard would it be to just let her be healthy?

She wanted to be the one that ran on the beach hand-in-hand with her boyfriend and thought about marriage and babies. But she wasn't going to have that.

And she really hated the fact that she couldn't be normal.

"They say that I'm too young, but my doctor thinks that I might need to have a hysterectomy soon. It's all just a bit too much on my body. Just another organ for the lupus to attack. Another place for toxins to build up. They think I'll start to feel better once it's gone."

Liam sat back, his eyes wide. He had gone a little pale,

and Arden wanted to scream. She just wanted to make everything better.

But she wasn't sure how to do that.

How on Earth could she do that?

"Are you feeling okay?" Liam asked, his voice steady.

"I mean, just pain. But that's all you have to say? You're asking if I'm feeling okay? I just told you that I might not ever be able to have kids. That they're going to take that choice from me. And I don't know how to feel about that."

"I don't know either," he said softly and then touched her face, resting his forehead against hers.

"All I know is that I'm here for you, okay? I'm here. You don't have to make any decisions right now. You don't even have to think about it. You just need to rest up and get one part of you better. And then you can take care of the rest. And I know we haven't talked about family or anything, mostly because we're still pretty new at what we are now, but if we go down that road? Then we will. And, hell, we were just talking to Austin about adoption, right? I mean, I know we're not there yet, nowhere close, but I'm not going to walk away just because of this. Okay? I promise. So, you don't have to worry about me. This is all you. Okay?"

She nodded, sinking into his hold as he scooted her over on the bed so they could sit together.

It was a little weight off her shoulders, just a bit off her chest.

But the rest of it? She had to focus on that. She hadn't ever really known if she wanted kids, but the idea that she couldn't give birth to any of her own? Well, that…that had been on her mind. Because her body hated her. And while she could feel mostly healthy for eighty percent of her life and find ways around the pain, there would always be times when her body laughed at her.

"I just don't know what to think," she whispered.

"Then don't think, you don't have to think about it right now. You just need to get better, and then we'll take the next step. I know there are people you can talk to. Those who've been through what you have or something similar. Maybe we can find them." He was so quiet for a moment, Arden was sure he was done, but then he continued. "And I know I'm not always good with words, though sometimes I am. I just…I want you to know that I'm here. Always."

She leaned into him, knowing that he was serious, realizing that he was truthful.

And she couldn't help but wonder when she was going to catch a break. Just a little one.

But she was in the arms of the man that she loved, her family was healthy, and she was going to be okay. What she had wasn't too serious. She was managing it. She was going to be fine.

And when they found the right cocktail of drugs, she would be back to her usual, happy self.

It was just when it all came at her one thing after another like this? It was a lot.

But she would be fine.

Because she had to be.

CHAPTER 21

*L*iam typed away on the computer as Arden slept, her face peaceful in repose.

They were going to let her go home the next morning, and he was grateful for that.

The pancreatitis hadn't been as bad as they feared, and she had caught it early because she knew her body, and everyone was grateful for that, too.

Liam had just been so damn scared.

He hated that seeing her in a hospital bed was starting to become routine. She and her brothers had promised him that it wasn't always like this, that these just happened to be a tough couple of months. He was going to let that soothe him.

He hated the fact that Arden was in pain. And there was nothing he could do other than be there for her.

So, he just watched her sleep and then went back to his computer, trying to finish up the last part of his book.

Seeing Arden in pain, watching her cry for what she might lose had made him discover the ending of his book.

He knew exactly what it needed to say, knew precisely what it needed to be.

Because of Arden.

It was always because of Arden.

He had met her when everything changed. When he'd thought he knew who he was and found out that he really didn't.

Because he wasn't just a man who had lost everything. Because he hadn't really. He had gained something, too. An idea that he was different.

And all because of his family and the woman that slept in front of him.

Nash worried so much about saving the world and what was in front of him that sometimes he forgot where he came from.

And that was something Liam had forgotten, as well.

Because while he had told himself that he would never forget where he had come from, he truly had.

He doubted himself and the fact that he was a Montgomery.

Even when he'd said that he knew adoptions took

place and everything was just fine, he had doubted himself.

He had doubted his family.

But they loved him even more fiercely now than before. And, yes, there would always be some twinges and weirdness with it, but that wasn't what made him...him.

What made him who he was, was how he had been raised and who he'd become.

So, he was going to push the thoughts of birth fathers and weirdness out of his mind. Maybe forever. The other Montgomerys in other cities could know if they wanted, but it didn't matter to him. It couldn't. Not when there were more important things in the world.

Mainly? The woman in front of him.

And that was how he knew he could write Nash's story.

Because his hero needed to be vulnerable. Yes, his body had been so for most of the series. He had been stabbed and thrown off buildings and almost blown up.

He'd had to hide from killers and had to kill people himself.

All physical—except for maybe the latter.

But he'd never had to be truly vulnerable.

And Penny made him that way.

So, Liam was going to have to figure out what came next.

Because Nash needed to say that he loved Penny. That he was going to give everything up for her if that's what she wanted.

Liam sighed and looked down at the screen, knowing he needed to finish the book.

Because it wasn't just Nash and Penny.

It was Arden.

"It's always you," he whispered.

Because Arden had never been a distraction despite what he'd tried to tell himself. He fucking loved her.

He never wanted to lose her.

And he was so afraid that if he weren't careful, he might.

He kept working, opening Nash up in a way that he never had before.

Maybe his readers wouldn't like it, but perhaps they needed it.

Because there had to be hope in the darkness.

Even if Nash and Penny went on their next adventure together, rather than apart.

But Nash needed to know that he could lose everything, and Penny needed to know that Nash would throw away everything for her, and vice versa.

Liam wrote for a good hour, saving as much as he could, even plugging in his computer to the outlet the nurses had shown him he was allowed to use. He just typed away, so much so that when he finally looked up again and blinked, he found Arden silently looking at him, a smile on her face.

"Hey, I didn't know you were awake," he said quickly, hitting save before rolling back his shoulders.

"Just watching you work. I like watching you work."

Liam grinned.

"I look like I'm insane. I slowly tilt my head to the side and have to straighten myself up when I find myself practically horizontal. I mouth the words when I type sometimes, and I make random facial expressions depending on the mood of the character."

"Yes, you do, but how did you know that?"

"Because I filmed myself once after Ethan watched me write and made fun of me. I was convinced there was no way my brother was right."

"Of course, because little brothers are never right."

"No, Aaron's the baby brother. And he's never right. Ethan, well, he's right a lot of the time, but we don't like to talk about that."

"So, you taped yourself?"

"Yep. And it was as bad as Ethan said. I'm a mess. But I know I'm not alone." He winked at her, and she laughed.

"Oh?"

"I've watched you work. That day we worked side by side on the couch, and the other when we went outside when we wanted a bit of sun. You do the same things I do."

"Oh, really? No wonder I'm always sore after working."

"It's hell on our bodies."

"Yeah, so are a lot of things."

They were silent for a moment, not touching, just looking at each other.

Arden was going to be okay, that much he knew, because there really wasn't another option.

And he wasn't going anywhere. No matter what. He would be by her side.

Because he had found something worth fighting for. Someone.

And it had nothing to do with where he had come from, it was where he was going.

And that was towards Arden.

He hadn't been looking for her, but he had found her regardless.

"What were you writing?" Arden asked. "Can you finally tell me what Nash decides?"

Liam let out a breath and nodded. "Let me read it to you."

Her eyes widened, and she leaned forward.

He wasn't surprised that she looked a little off-kilter. After all, he was very private with his work. He didn't like having anyone see it before he revised it.

And she had only seen his work after it was ready for publication.

But this was different.

Because Nash and Penny were for her.

"You see, I'm at the point where Nash is deciding what he needs to do when it comes to Penny, his work, and his future."

"Okay," she said softly, nodding. "Do I need to know what happens at the beginning of the book?"

"Not right now. It's just you and me, okay? Just this part."

And so he told her about Nash's artifact, and how Nash and Penny had figured out their ending and how to save the world. And also that Nash had figured out his future. No matter how many times he had to save the world, there was only one path for him. The one with Penny. He told her that Nash had finally made his choice. And in the end, there was only one. There was only ever one.

And then Liam looked up at her and spoke Nash's words. He didn't need to read them to know what they were. After all, he had just written them down, and they were engraved on his heart. "I never thought I'd fall. Never thought I needed to. But there are no nets, no safety, no staying tied and thinking I'm free. I love you. With everything that I have. Don't push me away. Let me stay." He paused, swallowing hard as Arden wiped tears from her cheeks. "Let me stay. Let me love you."

CHAPTER 22

*A*rden swallowed hard, wiping tears from her cheeks. "Did Nash really say that? Because that's wonderful for Penny."

Liam closed his laptop, set it on the counter next to him, and then stood up to stand next to Arden's hospital bed. "Yes, it's Nash. But it's not just Nash, and you know that."

Her hands shook, and she reached out to cup his face. "I love you, too," she whispered.

He loved her. And he had told her in the best way possible. He had spun them both together in a cacophony of promise, written in his beautiful words. Unique, just like how they had met. Like how they knew each other far beyond just a meeting in a park or in a hospital.

Nash loved Penny, and Liam loved her.

"I love you," she whispered.

"I'm always going to want to hear that. Always," he growled. "And I really wish you weren't in a hospital bed, because I think there is something that I want to do to you right now to prove that."

She snorted and shook her head. "Unlike in certain TV shows, sex in a hospital is gross. Think of all the germs."

"Yeah, totally not going to do that here. But when we get home? When you feel better? Totally going to do you."

She snorted, laughing hard. "Now that's romantic. Do me?"

"Make sweet love to you while rose petals fall over us and candles are lit."

"For a writer, you don't really have much imagination. What if the petals fall on the candlesticks and catch fire, and then set the curtains on fire, and then everything's on fire, but we're too busy making out, and Jasper just leaves us going...*whatever*."

Liam was full-out laughing at that point, and she was too. He kissed away her tears. But they were happy tears. Finally, happy tears.

"You're such a dork. But you're my dork."

"You're a dork. I really like that. So, this is us, then? Love and sparkles and all the good things?"

"Sparkles?" he asked, taking a seat next to her as he

wiped her face with his thumbs. He was getting good at that, and she only wanted happy tears from now on. Even though she knew sad ones would come, they always did, she wanted to be happy.

And he made her happy.

And the fact that she was his? That made all of this worth it.

"I'm just saying, you have to know what you're in for," she said quickly, sobering just a bit. "I'm going to have good days and bad days. I just hope there're more good days. But no matter what, I want all my days with you."

Liam blinked at her, kissed her hard, and then grinned. "I think I'm going to need to put that in a book."

She shoved at his chest, but he didn't back away. "I'm going to need royalties for that then."

He laughed, pressed his lips to hers, and she melted into him.

"I love you so much. And I told you, I'm not going away. So, no matter what, you're going to have to deal with me in your life. All of us Montgomerys, actually."

She grinned and leaned into him. "You're going to have to deal with the Bradys, too."

"Dear God, the force of the two families together? There's nothing we can't do."

They kissed again, and only stopped when the nurse came in and cleared his throat.

No, they were not on a certain medical TV show, so

Liam went back to his book, and she just watched him write and fell in love with him even more.

Thankfully, they let her out of the hospital the next day as promised, and she was back to feeling normal—whatever normal was for her.

There would be decisions to come, and there would be surgeries most likely. But they had time. She had time.

And she wasn't worried. Because no matter what the decisions were, she wasn't going to make them alone.

Yes, it was her body, her health, but she had someone to talk to. And not just family.

She had Liam.

She wrapped her arms around her dog. Jasper licked her face, and she grinned.

Well, she had Liam and Jasper. She had her men, she had the idea of her future.

She couldn't wait to see what happened next, because she wasn't alone.

They weren't going to walk away from her.

She had been through enough in her life to know when things were true and steady. And they were. Liam and Jasper were her rocks.

She didn't know what would happen next, but she couldn't wait to find out.

Because she had fallen in love with Liam Montgomery. Through one smile, one cup of coffee, and one blue-faced dog, she had fallen in love.

And love, as they said, could heal anything.

Even when she'd thought she had lost her hope in the darkness.

EPILOGUE

*I*t had taken a couple of months, but they were finally having a Montgomery dinner where Arden was involved. Between illnesses, hospital visits, people going out of town for work, going out of the country, and secret babies—something that he and Arden liked to talk about between them because laughing about something rather than crying about it was sort of how they made their lives work—they hadn't actually been able to do the big dinner with Arden.

Their lives were immensely busy, and most of them ended up having to travel long distances when they were done with their work at home.

Liam himself had a book tour coming up, and he was trying to convince Arden to come with him.

Yes, the world was finally going to see his face, even though they had already quietly put it up on his website and social media.

He had a feeling that pretty boy modeling photos would show up at any moment, but he didn't care.

He just wanted Arden by his side when he traveled the country, talking about Nash's new book.

The one that came out next year where Nash and Penny finally professed their feelings for each other as they continued to save the world together? That was the book he was really excited about. But first, he wanted to go on tour with the woman who had saved his world.

He would get her to agree. Eventually.

Bristol had just gotten back from a trip to France where she had played for some dignitaries or celebrities or something. She hadn't been really forthcoming about it since she had been kind of embarrassed, but they all had the video set up to watch her play later after dinner, just in case.

Sometimes, she wasn't in the mood and felt way too self-conscious, but it was fun to praise his baby sister.

Aaron had come home from another showing of his work, but was quiet as usual, probably contemplating his next piece of art.

Ethan, of course, was always home, but he was the brilliant one, the sibling constantly in his mind, and didn't travel much.

He was there with the rest of them tonight.

And he had brought his friend Lincoln.

Lincoln was practically a Montgomery since he and Ethan were as thick as thieves.

Liam was close to Lincoln, as well, but Ethan was the same age as Linc.

Lincoln had been off for some showing or other since he was a famous painter, which just made Liam smile.

So many artists in the family. And then there was Ethan, the brainiac. Liam loved it.

He put his arm around Arden and looked around at his family. He couldn't believe that they were here. All of them.

Yes, there would always be that little bit of tension when he first walked into a room, but hopefully, that would go away eventually.

Because he had chosen his loyalties. His family.

After all, they had chosen him.

He was a Montgomery, through and through.

As Ethan and Lincoln laughed at something his mother said, Liam just shook his head.

Their mother loved Lincoln like a son, and she was always trying to get him to marry Bristol—if Bristol didn't marry Marcus.

Not that Bristol wanted either of them.

It was just that Francine Montgomery really wanted grandbabies. It seemed since the other Montgomerys had all started having children, his mom needed some, as well.

Liam squeezed Arden's shoulders, and she looked up at him. He didn't say anything. They weren't going to mention the fact that when and if they decided to have children in the future, they would go the adoption route.

That really wasn't anyone's business, much like his birth father wasn't anyone's business.

He had a feeling if he had his way, and if Arden moved forward with how they had been speaking lately, maybe one day soon there would be a baby or an older child for Francine to spoil like grandmothers do.

One step at a time, though.

Bristol was in the corner, arguing with Marcus about something, and Liam just rolled his eyes. The two of them weren't laughing about some plan they were in on, they were arguing.

How the two ended up best friends for so long was beyond him.

But everyone was there, all of them parts of the whole with their own dramas, but always there for each other. Always family.

Liam had almost forgotten that.

And because he had, he knew he needed to remember the true meaning of what had brought them all together.

"What are you over there overanalyzing," Ethan said, glaring at Liam.

Liam held up his free arm and shook his head. "You're the analytical one."

"But you're the one looking all weird in the corner and hugging Arden so close that you're hogging her."

"She's right, son," Francine said. "I haven't even been able to show Arden your baby pictures. And there're so many. There's one of him on an actual bearskin rug with his little tushy up in the air, and he's all smiles."

"Dear God, not the baby pictures."

"Eh, the baby pictures are old school. Show the modeling photos. With his pouty lips."

Ethan threw back his head and laughed at Aaron's words, then nodded.

"Yes, pouty lips! Pouty lips!" Ethan started chanting, and the rest of them joined in.

Liam pinched the bridge of his nose.

"Please, do not pull out those photos."

"Oh, the ones online?" Arden asked. She shook her head, laughing. "I already saw those. I didn't see the bearskin rug, though."

"I was an infant."

"Oh, I bet you were cute. Do you have other pouty lip photos? Maybe ones where he's giving like that blue steel face?" she asked and moved away from Liam's arm so she could follow his mother.

"You are all traitors," Liam ground out.

"You're the one who brought the new lamb to the

slaughter," Ethan said, grinning. "After all, none of us brought our significant others. We just brought friends. You're the one who brought the girlfriend. The one you loooove." He drawled out the word, and Liam rolled his eyes.

"One day, you will find someone that you love, and you'll bring them to dinner, and I will do everything within my power to embarrass you. You will rue the day."

"You know, no one uses that phrase enough these days," Ethan said, and Lincoln just shook his head, taking a sip of his beer.

"You really shouldn't egg him on," he whispered to Ethan. "You know, Liam was right with us with those pranks when we were kids. He's downright dastardly."

"See? No one uses that word either," Ethan said, laughing. "Plus, he can't do anything to us. It's not like any of us are in relationships."

Something flashed over Lincoln's gaze, and Liam's brows rose.

Interesting.

Very interesting.

Well, it seemed the rest of his family had secrets, and now that Liam had the love of his life by his side, and he was pretty sure that he had no more skeletons in his closet, he was just going to have to figure out what was going on with the rest of his family.

One Montgomery at a time.

THE END

Next in the Montgomery Ink: Boulder series?

It's Ethan's turn in SATED IN INK.

A NOTE FROM CARRIE ANN RYAN

Thank you so much for reading **WRAPPED IN INK.** I do hope if you liked this story, that you would please leave a review! Reviews help authors *and* readers.

I love the Montgomerys. I truly do. And these Boulder Montgomerys are so amazing and dare I say...bolder. Yes, I've been making that joke to myself while even writing hard topics.

As someone with an autoimmune disease, writing Arden's romance was a bit personal, but finding her HEA was perfect. Liam? Liam is a Montgomery. His personal journey into figuring that out is what made him a Montgomery.

As for who is next? Ethan is next though he's not going to go about it the usual away. I cannot wait for you to read his story.

Bristol and Aaron will be getting their stories as well!

And how about those Brady Brothers? You guessed it, I fell in love. I didn't mean to. But now they are getting a series of their own in the Promise Me series!

And if you're new to my books, you can start anywhere within the my interconnected series and catch up! Each book is a stand alone, so jump around!

Don't miss out on the Montgomery Ink World!

- Montgomery Ink (The Denver Montgomerys)
- Montgomery Ink: Colorado Springs (The Colorado Springs Montgomery Cousins)
- Montgomery Ink: Boulder (The Boulder Montgomery Cousins)
- Gallagher Brothers (Jake's Brothers from Ink Enduring)
- Whiskey and Lies (Tabby's Brothers from Ink Exposed)
- Fractured Connections (Mace's sisters from Fallen Ink)
- Less Than (Dimitri's siblings from Restless Ink)
- Promise Me (Arden's siblings from Wrapped in Ink)

If you want to make sure you know what's coming next from me, you can sign up for my newsletter at www. CarrieAnnRyan.com; follow me on twitter at @Carrie-

AnnRyan, or like my Facebook page. I also have a Facebook Fan Club where we have trivia, chats, and other goodies. You guys are the reason I get to do what I do and I thank you.

Make sure you're signed up for my MAILING LIST so you can know when the next releases are available as well as find giveaways and FREE READS.

Happy Reading!

The Montgomery Ink: Boulder Series:
Book 1: Wrapped in Ink
Book 2: Sated in Ink
Book 3: Embraced in Ink

Want to keep up to date with the next Carrie Ann Ryan Release? Receive Text Alerts easily!
Text CARRIE to 24587

ABOUT THE AUTHOR

Carrie Ann Ryan is the New York Times and USA Today bestselling author of contemporary, paranormal, and young adult romance. Her works include the Montgomery Ink, Redwood Pack, Fractured Connections, and Elements of Five series, which have sold over 3.0 million books worldwide. She started writing while in graduate school for her advanced degree in chemistry and hasn't stopped since. Carrie Ann has written over seventy-five novels and novellas with more in the works. When she's not losing herself in her emotional and action-packed worlds, she's reading as much as she can while wrangling her clowder of cats who have more followers than she does.

www.CarrieAnnRyan.com

The Montgomery Ink: Boulder Series:
Book 1: Wrapped in Ink
Book 2: Sated in Ink
Book 3: Embraced in Ink

The Less Than Series:
A Montgomery Ink Spin Off Series
Book 1: Breathless With Her
Book 2: Reckless With You
Book 3: Shameless With Him

The Elements of Five Series:
Book 1: From Breath and Ruin
Book 2: From Flame and Ash
Book 3: From Spirit and Binding

The Promise Me Series:

A Montgomery Ink Spin Off Series

Book 1: Forever Only Once

Book 2: From That Moment

The Fractured Connections Series:

A Montgomery Ink Spin Off Series

Book 1: Breaking Without You

Book 2: Shouldn't Have You

Book 3: Falling With You

Book 4: Taken With You

Montgomery Ink: Colorado Springs

Book 1: Fallen Ink

Book 2: Restless Ink

Book 2.5: Ashes to Ink

Book 3: Jagged Ink

Book 3.5: Ink by Numbers

Montgomery Ink:

Book 0.5: Ink Inspired

Book 0.6: Ink Reunited

Book 1: Delicate Ink

Book 1.5: Forever Ink

Book 2: Tempting Boundaries

Book 3: Harder than Words

Book 4: Written in Ink

Book 4.5: Hidden Ink
Book 5: Ink Enduring
Book 6: Ink Exposed
Book 6.5: Adoring Ink
Book 6.6: Love, Honor, & Ink
Book 7: Inked Expressions
Book 7.3: Dropout
Book 7.5: Executive Ink
Book 8: Inked Memories
Book 8.5: Inked Nights
Book 8.7: Second Chance Ink

The Gallagher Brothers Series:
A Montgomery Ink Spin Off Series
Book 1: Love Restored
Book 2: Passion Restored
Book 3: Hope Restored

The Whiskey and Lies Series:
A Montgomery Ink Spin Off Series
Book 1: Whiskey Secrets
Book 2: Whiskey Reveals
Book 3: Whiskey Undone

The Talon Pack:
Book 1: Tattered Loyalties
Book 2: An Alpha's Choice

Book 3: Mated in Mist
Book 4: Wolf Betrayed
Book 5: Fractured Silence
Book 6: Destiny Disgraced
Book 7: Eternal Mourning
Book 8: Strength Enduring
Book 9: Forever Broken

Redwood Pack Series:
Book 1: An Alpha's Path
Book 2: A Taste for a Mate
Book 3: Trinity Bound
Redwood Pack Box Set (Contains Books 1-3)
Book 3.5: A Night Away
Book 4: Enforcer's Redemption
Book 4.5: Blurred Expectations
Book 4.7: Forgiveness
Book 5: Shattered Emotions
Book 6: Hidden Destiny
Book 6.5: A Beta's Haven
Book 7: Fighting Fate
Book 7.5: Loving the Omega
Book 7.7: The Hunted Heart
Book 8: Wicked Wolf
The Complete Redwood Pack Box Set (Contains Books 1-7.7)

The Branded Pack Series:

(Written with Alexandra Ivy)

Book 1: Stolen and Forgiven

Book 2: Abandoned and Unseen

Book 3: Buried and Shadowed

Dante's Circle Series:

Book 1: Dust of My Wings

Book 2: Her Warriors' Three Wishes

Book 3: An Unlucky Moon

The Dante's Circle Box Set (Contains Books 1-3)

Book 3.5: His Choice

Book 4: Tangled Innocence

Book 5: Fierce Enchantment

Book 6: An Immortal's Song

Book 7: Prowled Darkness

The Complete Dante's Circle Series (Contains Books 1-7)

Holiday, Montana Series:

Book 1: Charmed Spirits

Book 2: Santa's Executive

Book 3: Finding Abigail

The Holiday, Montana Box Set (Contains Books 1-3)

Book 4: Her Lucky Love

Book 5: Dreams of Ivory

<u>The Complete Holiday, Montana Box Set</u> (Contains Books 1-5)

The Happy Ever After Series:
<u>Flame and Ink</u>
<u>Ink Ever After</u>

Single Title:
<u>Finally Found You</u>

CPSIA information can be obtained
at www.ICGtesting.com
Printed in the USA
LVHW051925300819
629530LV00010B/756